BURIED VAPORS

BURIED VAPORS

MATTHEW KESSELMAN

Published in 2020 by Novel Novels, an imprint of Novel Novels LLC

ISBN 9781952974007 (paperback)

ISBN 9781952974021 (hardcover)

ISBN 9781952974014 (ebook)

matthewkesselman.com

novelnovels.com

Dedicated to my Ma

CHAPTER ONE

I t was ugly. Maybe one of the ugliest things he had ever seen. Time had turned a sea of pure white into a sickly gray, hinting at dust settled deep within. The corners had become discolored—one had a dark-yellow stain, another a brownish-red tint—while the foam trapped underneath had developed abnormal dents, like subtle trenches sketching out the weight of lives lived before. It had faced time and lost. Its suffering, its decay, were undeniable. Yet even in this state, it refused to die. Instead it would survive under a new master.

In front of Ian was his mattress. *What an ugly thing*, he thought.

THE PREVIOUS NIGHT, Ian slept on the floor.

After a rushed search, he had been fortunate enough to find two whole rooms in the City. In a way, it was an impressive sight: an entrance, bedroom, and kitchen all crammed into one 200-square-foot rectangle. *And* a bathroom. However, unfortunately for Ian, it still lacked some furniture.

As he lay on the floor, planks creaked and his shoulders

chaffed, but in the discomfort he found a trace of joy. Above the hardwood, wrapped in the dark, his mind was free to wander. It conjured up ancient memories from boyhood, times when he would lie on grass and spend all night staring at an illuminated sky. He could remember imagined worlds that used to be his playgrounds, adventures where he would walk among the stars or fly to new galaxies, go anywhere his heart desired. That night, just for one night, he could taste a life when the world was still new, an era he had forgotten, when anything was possible and time was infinite, as he was carried into a dreamless sleep.

In the morning, his back groaned. He rubbed it, watched a video labeled "How to Meet People in a New City," and prepared to leave. He needed to see his cousin Lizzy.

She was distant, Ian's mother's sister's husband's brother's daughter, and they had only met twice before, despite living only an hour's distance apart for most of their lives. Their most recent encounter, twelve years earlier at an aunt's birthday party, had ended abruptly. She called him weird; he said her puffy hair looked silly. She annoyed him; he ignored her. Then, out of frustration, she stole his slice of cake, ran away, and gobbled it down in three bites, while Ian watched.

He had never forgiven, simply forgotten.

Before Ian knew he was moving, he had forgotten everything: the little girl, her messy hair, the robbery. Her name and face no longer seemed to even be true memories, more like lost droplets in a sea of neurons, never to be excavated, adrift forever. Yet, in an instant, his mom brought it all back. She told him Lizzy was living in the City. She would be his only family there. Call her.

Faster than the time it took for him to blink, he had evaporated the hidden liquid and relived dead experiences. They whispered "*avoid her*," but after questioning himself once or twice, he caved. He had texted her a month earlier but received no follow-up. Then he sent another text, which also went nowhere.

Ian had stared at his phone, feeling uneasy about tapping in the digits. He had only called four distinct people over the last few months, and even those people he preferred to text.

"Hi, Lizzy? It's—"

"Hello? Who is this?"

"It's Ian—"

"Who? I don't know an Ian."

"Your cousin, I'm moving near you… I think your mom may have told you. I called to catch up."

"Ian… Ian… Oh yes, Ian! You messaged me, right? Oh my god! I didn't know you were coming here!"

"That's right. I just finished school and I found a job—"

"That's great. So exciting. We need to catch up. By the way, do you want some furniture?"

It turned out Lizzy was moving as well, to live with her boyfriend, and she needed to get rid of any trace of her old junk as soon as possible. Ian would be her lucky recipient.

The instructions to find her apartment had been clear: fourteen stops, one subway, one street. Stepping outside, Ian lifted his chest and breathed in frigid air. As he walked to the train, the City's energy radiated all around him. Pedestrians rustled past one another at breakneck speeds, forming an invisible, pulsating electricity powered by their cumulative ambition, hope, and doubt.

He decided it was time to find his way, time to begin a new chapter. He took a step, and another, journeying down into the subway station… and instantly became lost. First, wrong station. Then, wrong train. No, actually, wrong direction.

The sprawling underground proved too much to swallow all at once. He had abandoned his old worn car in a long-term parking lot outside of the City in exchange for steel snakes screeching and sliding twenty-four hours a day. Born of a place where the weather was warm and the days long, the City made him feel like he was living in a stranger.

But after the initial struggle, he found his path. During the journey's first ten stops, the subway moved a hundred feet below street level, and he watched a somber story play on loop in its windows. Between stations, the train's glass panes stayed pitch black, masked by sunken earth save the occasional revolt. The train moved so fast it was as if fluorescent lamps flashed, shining bright for a moment, cutting through the dark, before their light disappeared forever.

However, as the trip approached its eleventh stop, there was a revolution. The train climbed out of the underground and carried its passengers into the light of the neighborhood, which revealed its life to Ian. He gazed at a hodgepodge of dirty red-brick buildings, none bigger than seven stories. On one corner there was a 99-cent store, next to it, a Pollo Feliz, across from those, a Salon Barber Shop, and crammed in a corner, Delicias Puebla. The street resembled a turbulent engine, with people coming and going, moving left and right. Riding above the earth, he saw countless stories in perpetual motion, all inter-woven yet unknown to each other.

He wondered where they were all going.

As the train screeched to its stop, he spotted Lizzy's apartment building across the street. Then the doors opened, and the flood of humanity flowed. Ian managed to squeeze his way out, while the other departees shoved their way out. After his escape, he regained his bearings and went left. He clanked down hollow metal steps, and once he reached the street, he looked back up at the train's platform. It dominated the block, casting its shadow across the neighborhood and upon the pedestrians who crawled beneath it.

The ground beneath him began to rumble, and he spotted another train coming into the station. It entered on a difficult curve and had no qualms complaining about it. As it turned, it blared, shrieking and snarling, clashing metal against metal, sending small golden sparks flying into the air.

Within seconds the hum in the ground grew into a shake that pushed him back and forced him to catch his balance, until it all slowed to a smooth stop.

It appeared the City dictated even the earth's tune.

When he reached Lizzy's apartment building's gate he buzzed in for 3E, waited, and buzzed again. After some more waiting he pulled out his phone, but then the lock yielded and he swung the gate open.

The entrance was a thin dim hallway with a staircase, an elevator, and just two doors at the end of the wall. Its tightness gave Ian a sudden urge to leave, so he jogged up the stairs, turned a corner, and there, holding her door open, was Lizzy. She hadn't changed a bit: She looked as silly as ever and her hair was still a tangled mess. She offered a toothy grin and a hug.

"Welcome!"

He gave her a half hug back. "It's good to see you."

"Come inside," she said.

As he stepped in and scanned the space, a wave of unease drifted up his spine. The living room had succumbed to entropy, engulfed in a final collapse of complete chaos. The floor was a minefield of clothes, the coffee table had been transformed into a tower of mismatched shoes, and a half-eaten pizza crust teetered on the brink of disaster, resting dangerously atop a flimsy paper plate above the couch's armrest.

"Sorry for the mess," Lizzy said. "There was a lot of life to move."

Lizzy led Ian into the apartment's sole bedroom. The scene was a little better, mostly because it was already emptied. All that remained were four clean white walls, a barren wooden floor, an assortment of boxes, a small black desk, a shelf, a frail chair, a bed frame, and a naked mattress.

"What do you think?" Lizzy asked.

Ian leaned down and stroked the mattress's soft surface, then tested it. He pushed, pressing as much as his strength would allow. It choked under his weight, but when he released his grip, it easily bounced back to proper form. He decided its ugliness didn't matter; it would be enough. Big, strong, and free. "It'll work," he said.

Slowly, then suddenly, all the pieces rattled, followed by the whole room, and finally Ian's feet. He fell over, rolling onto the bed.

"Sorry about that," she said, standing straight. "Living so close to the train has had its disadvantages. You get used to it, but I'm so ready to move. I need better sleep."

"Gotcha," said Ian. "Thanks again. I appreciate the help."

Lizzy looked at him and shrugged. "It's fine. I inherited it all from the previous tenant anyways. I never used most of it, except the bed."

They lifted the furniture into Lizzy's red sedan, which had a dent stretched across its front passenger door. As they rolled block by block, Ian could feel the mattress, precariously attached to the car's roof, bouncing at every pothole.

They did not speak during the drive. Instead the City watched Ian. There was no escaping it. The skyline proved beyond anything he had ever seen. Mesmerizing, all-encompassing, magnificently terrifying.

Once they arrived, she helped him unload the desk, the shelf, and finally, the mattress. She shoved it off the roof, and it flipped, landing in front of Ian's feet, staring up at its new owner and a gray sky. Then she grumbled "I hope you enjoy it" before scurrying away.

Ian spent the next five minutes dragging the furniture up his stoop. An older man walking out of the building spotted

Ian's predicament and stopped to hold open the gate. Ian slid through and pulled the furniture the rest of the way.

"Thanks," said Ian, but the man didn't respond. He was already gone.

After he stuffed everything into the elevator, shoved it into his tiny apartment, and tossed the mattress onto the bedframe, Ian paused for a moment. He examined the mattress's seams and crevices and stains, then collapsed onto the bed.

First he lay flat, exhausted, but began to roll, trying to find a more comfortable position. However, something rubbed against the back of his head. He propped himself up and turned to the exposed mattress and frowned. There was a tiny tear on the mattress's surface, near its top, revealing aged yellow foam hidden underneath. It must have ripped after Lizzy shoved it onto the ground, he decided. A shame.

For hours, he watched more videos on his phone. "Top 7 Ways to Make Side Money NOW," then "How to Get Over the End of a Relationship," and then "6 Minutes to Start Your Day Right!" Then, in the middle of his distractions, he received a message with a payment request attached: *$150 — Gas and other stuff, bed is free. Sorry that the boyfriend couldn't help :/*

Ian stared at it for a bit, then pressed the accept button.

Work was to begin in a couple days. How much sleep would he get once it started, he wondered.

He crawled forward on the bed toward the window, his only window, a tiny square that revealed a slice of the world beyond. Near him were a line of buildings, all too close and too tall for him to be able to see their tops, and above them the true heroes of the City, the skyscrapers, continued to rule. They spoke to their peons through wind and steel, through shadow and power.

Below them, on the street, Ian spotted dozens, maybe hundreds, of pedestrians walking, darting forward and back in a perpetual frenzy. And farthest beyond, peeking through a crevice between buildings, the sun watched him. It was falling for the night, taking shelter behind the maze of the mighty City.

He witnessed it all on his phone's display as he took a picture.

Yawning, he scanned the image. Then he leaned over and flipped off the light. He would brush his teeth tomorrow.

Into twilight, Ian scrolled on his phone, hopping from experience to experience, until the device died in his hands hours later. He put it aside and finally faced the night.

Staring into the cold dark, stewing over the near future, he tried to imagine what would become of him, what his new life would yield, but he could find only uncertainty. It was as though a hidden glow that had once illuminated his life's path was now dimming to black, leaving nothing behind but a murky fog for him to crawl into, while everyone else in the City raced ahead.

He stopped, listened. The room had become too quiet. He rolled over and plugged his phone into the charger and closed his eyes.

Some stray light kept trickling in from the window, but soon it faded. In complete darkness sleep came easy.

Thump. Thump. Thump.

Ian placed his hands on the top of his head and held it gently. It pulsated in slow, melodic beats.

Then it throbbed.

Thump! Thump! Thump!

He pressed his hands down onto his skull. The inside of his head banged like the echo of a drum smashed by a steel baton, feeling as if it could burst at any moment. He tried to open his eyes, but the effort proved impossible. Even the smallest bit of light stung and burned; everything was far too bright, nothing was clear.

After mechanically forcing his eyelids up with his hands, one after the other, he received a blurred vision of the world around him, a chaotic tumble of blue, gray, green, and white, all fused together.

Their shine only brought more confusion, and difficulty in concentration. He couldn't make out a single smell; his sinuses were stuffed. He could barely feel; his hands were numb. Around him could have been stone and sea or sky and spires. Or simply cement.

Frustrated, he blinked, until he finally found a minor break-through. He could make out the shapes of trees close by and the outlines of buildings in the distance.

He cried out, "Hello?"

There was no response except the gentle hum of cars rolling by, somewhere out of sight. He waited for an answer as a tremor grew in his heart. He opened his mouth, prepared to yell again, when he heard a murmur.

"Ma, I did it."

Like a blind man, he whipped his head toward the sound. It was a strong voice, a man's voice, one that should have arrived with a boom, hitting deep and low. But in this blurred world the stranger had changed. He spoke slower, quieter, and cautiously. *Weaker*.

Only a few yards away, Ian saw his dark, blurred profile, but he could not make him out. "Who are you?" he yelled.

The man gave no response. Instead his voice reverberated, "I don't know. It's been too quick. I don't know if she's the one. I bought the ring, I really did, but I just don't know."

Ian tried to move through his fog toward the voice; however, the moment he lifted his foot, his legs wobbled and collapsed, dumping his body onto the ground. He tumbled onto grass as soft as cotton, which caressed his hands and face. Propping himself up by his forearm, he watched the figure move farther away.

"What's going on?" asked Ian.

The man ignored him. He continued to walk forward and speak to the open air. He whispered, "I just don't know, Mama."

In his struggle, Ian began to feel nausea creeping up from the bottom of his stomach and spreading to his throat. He released his pose, fell back onto the grass, and stretched his neck up to gaze forward, until he could no longer make out the man. The dark blur had faded away, melted into the hazy horizon that dominated his vision.

He tried to push himself up again, but this time his arms completely failed him. He collapsed onto his side, rolled onto his back, and stared at the calm blue sky above him, where there was no sun delivering a blinding shine, nor a cloud to block his view. There on the ground, for a brief second, he found peace. His mind began to slow, to regain focus, and he almost tried to stand again. But then the moment vanished.

The sky flared, blasting a glow in all directions, like the light reflected off a diamond. The bright streaks zipped through the sky, forcing Ian to squint as they scattered across the heavens and dispersed into the universe. In their path they left behind thin white cuts slashed throughout the upper atmosphere.

After stillness had resumed, he held a sort of tension inside, waiting for something else to break, but finally it seemed to be over. He sighed and decided he would lay there forever. There was no need to get up. It was comfortable enough; the grass embraced his weary body and his tired mind, putting both at ease.

But it didn't last. It couldn't. Nothing did, Ian knew.

Watching the sky, he saw the glow's light fade away until the heavens reached an equilibrium once again, a warm, pure blue.

But then it flickered. The sky's color blinked into an absolute dark, devoid of stars or a moon to shine a path. Instead the heavens rested empty, leaving nothing behind but black.

Staring into the void, a nervous tremor returned to Ian's heart.

Using the remainder of his energy, he propped himself up. The mess of greens and grays around him also began to join the sky and fade into the cold darkness. They fell into the swallowing void as it chewed up any shapes, light, and life it could find.

Trembling, he felt the ground beneath him give away. Its soft grass turned to loose black, which turned into nothingness. It lost its tangibility and he began to slip.

At first the drop was a slow descent; the earth faded below his feet and his body dipped, gently pulling him down while he studied his dissolving world, wondering what midnight logic had delivered him such a sight.

Then he was plunged. The ground disappeared faster and faster, dragging everything, including Ian, down with it. He was crashing, diving, and was far too weak and too tired to scream. Instead all he managed to muster was a single pathetic whisper into the vacuum: "No."

Searching in the shadows, he once again spotted the figure of the dark man in the distance; he, too, was fading away.

"Okay, Mama. I'm ready," the man whispered before he disappeared entirely.

Then there seemed to be only silence, but Ian swore he could hear something, something metallic on the fringe of this empty reality. It was ever so subtle, just the sliver of a whisper, but it was there, he was certain of it. It was the sound of a distant train coming into a station.

Ian took in a breath through his mouth, sighed, and closed his eyes once again.

CHAPTER TWO

I an squeezed until his knuckles turned red and the plastic crimp cut into his palm, but soon he got his reward: a tiny bit of white toothpaste. It would have to be enough; he needed to leave soon. Although he had no idea of what he would be doing, it certainly sounded important. He was to be a "digital analyst."

In college, he had told his friends that he had simply applied, and it worked out, but that wasn't exactly accurate. As school was nearing its end, he would habitually search online: *how to find a job*. He did this almost every week but never quite got past the point of submitting an anemic resume into an online black hole before giving up. Fortunately, his father said he could help him. After all, Ian would need the cash flow to pay off his loans.

His father had a friend of a friend who worked in the City. He reached out on Ian's behalf, there was an interview, and the pieces fell into place.

When he had told his mom about the offer, she was giddy. She smiled and hugged him tight and said she was proud, while his father nodded and gave him an empty leather wallet as a gift. He told him, "Now it's your turn to fill it."

The mirror reflected back a collared shirt and slacks and unease, like a younger version of his father going to work, stuck somewhere between a child and an adult. An anxious chord twanged in the pit of Ian's belly.

Then he checked the time. 7:45 a.m. It was time to go, time to venture. He wanted to be sure to get there early.

First, open the door. Don't forget to lock the door. Press the elevator button. Wait. Wait longer. It was taking too long.

Down the staircase. Three flights. Three, two, one. Down the hallway. Open the door, out the door. Speed-walk down two blocks. Turn right. Find the entrance. Descend into the earth. Down, down, down into the earth. Wait for the train. Battle the rush to enter the train. Get bumped and battered.

Then, something new quietly arrived, a moment of stillness. Here, locked in the subway of a morning commute, time began to slow... until it stopped.

Momentarily, there was only the rhythmic hum of the train, the rustle of silent pedestrians, and the smooth electronic voice of a robot conductor whispering over the speaker system.

On the other side of the car, surrounded by the mob, was the side of a young woman's hat. She wore a green beanie that dripped lustrous brown hair, shining even in the underground car's dusk. Ian stared at her for a moment, lost in the instant.

Then she turned, sat, and became hidden by the crowd. And time resumed.

The train went down. Down. Down. Downtown. Zooming past stops, stops passed. Doors opened. Doors closed. Eight stops later, get spit out. Go left. Go right. Another left. Ascend out of the earth. Up, up, up out of the earth. Go straight. Two blocks. No, three. Go right. Stop.

Ian checked the time. 8:15 a.m.

. . .

Under the shadow of the skyscraper stood Ian. He had arrived at his company's office, a giant of steel and glass. Craning his neck, he made out the early trickle of laborers moving into their roles. Then he closed his eyes and listened. The hustle, the cars, and the wind all stacked on top of each other, forming a constant background buzz, a thick weight of sound that hung above the whole City.

The twinge of nervousness in his stomach had grown to a crescendo. He opened his eyes and watched the wide doors of the building's entrance open and close. The herd entered in droves, their footsteps crashing like waves against the concrete pavement. After a final hesitation, he moved to join them.

Once he reached his destination, the twenty-second floor, Ian was dumped out. He tumbled forward, then stopped.

In front of him stood a pasty man with dark black hair and a clean gray suit. On his left hand he wore a dull golden ring, and he had tired eyes, but they did not waver. Instead they held a concrete focus. Staring at Ian was the man who had interviewed him, his manager, Oscar.

Before the interview, Ian had done his research. When he first saw Oscar's picture, he thought he must be in his midfifties, but the truth was he was forty-six. Ian also found out that he had once played college basketball, but that reality had long dissipated. His strength had faded, his body had thinned, and he had paled.

In the interview, the first thing Ian noticed were the lin painted deep into his forehead. He had wondered if they w from surprise or worry, but he quickly realized he had them wrong—they were from intense energy. When C spoke, the words were frenzied, like he had too much with too little time to say it. When he became fired up, ignited and his youth returned, if only for a moment.

Oscar smiled, and Ian instinctively smiled bac smile was warm. "Hi, Ian. Let's go to my office."

Ian nodded and said nothing.

Oscar led him around one corner and down through a hall toward his office. Along the way, they passed the floor's open workspace, which featured long benches, modern computers, and massive windows, offering ample distractions. Ian spotted a few early birds pecking at emails from the week before, while other slugs began to slowly crawl. Their post-weekend bleariness needed more time to recede. Still, despite the contemporary trappings, he could not help but notice the chipped gray walls. They stood out, dripping awkward paint over the company's modernist composition, just enough to ruin it. Summed together, it seemed the future still needed more time to fully mask the past in present.

The two reached Oscar's office. "Please get comfortable," he said, closing the door. The room was a sleek space, and when Ian sat, his back rejoiced. The chairs were custom built with perfected ergonomics, designed to make one never want to stand again.

"I just wanted to say you're going to do a great job," Oscar said. He stared directly into Ian's eyes. Ian met them, then ꞁoked slightly down.

"Thanks, I appreciate that," said Ian as he looked up, not ꓸ Oscar, but to the world outside his full-length windows.
for this opportunity."

ꞁmiled again. "You're welcome." He paused. "It's
ꓸat." Then he rose. "You'll need to fill some stuff
'y will help you with that." He walked past Ian
ꞁr for him. "If you ever have a question, any
ꞁow."

ꞁll."

ꞁorning as a sheep. He flocked
ꓹ his tax forms, took a picture

for his ID, and was shepherded to his desk, where he was to wait to meet his team.

There, in front of a glowing screen, he hid while glancing around. Next to him was a young man with a trimmed beard that hugged tight cheekbones. He fidgeted, and when Ian realized that he intended to speak with him, Ian tried to look away, but it was too late. They had locked eyes, and the young man had already accepted the invitation.

He stood and asked, "Ian? Is that you?"

Reluctantly, Ian waved at him and rose as well.

He grinned. "It's good to meet you, man. I'm Rohan. We're working on the same project."

The two shook hands. Rohan's grip was stronger than Ian's.

"Let's go get lunch. Zoey will meet us there," Rohan said as he walked off. Ian followed, needing to speed up his step to keep pace. Rohan took long, hurried strides.

"So how has the move been? Do you like your place?"

"It's been okay," said Ian. "I think I just need to get used to it. I've become lost more than a couple times."

Rohan laughed. "Yeah, that'll happen. I moved here last year after I graduated, and the first week I ended up getting on the wrong train at least three times." The two entered an elevator with five others, so Rohan whispered, "I think you'll love it here. There's always something to do. At least I know I have."

In the cafeteria, Ian discovered his array of options: the salad or the sandwich. He chose the sandwich.

Rohan led him to a table where a woman sat with her back erect and her eyes laser focused. She was also young, though slightly older than Ian and Rohan. Ian looked at her with some curiosity and some apprehension. Her face was aggressively friendly, like she was always ready to start a conversation with a stranger, but one ultimately in her control.

She leaned over the table and gave Ian a soft handshake. "Hi, Ian, I'm Zoey."

"Hi, I'm Ian," he said as he sat across from her and Rohan.

"What do you think of everything so far?" she asked.

Ian paused. "I don't really know. I haven't really done anything."

They laughed, and Zoey gave a wide smile.

"I guess that's a good point," she said. "Well, we'll be working to redesign a client's user interface. It's a great, great project."

Rohan piped in, "It's for Paper Now. Papernow.com. They're an old paper company who started an online service. Their website is ancient and sales have dipped, so they came to us for a refresh."

"Ah, I see." Ian smiled. "Do they sell good paper?"

Rohan and Zoey glanced at each other. Rohan said, "I don't think we source our paper from them."

IAN SPENT the rest of the day reading, studying, and taking notes on every element of papernow.com. He was fed analysis after analysis and sucked it in until he knew every pixel, every function, and how to sell it.

Minutes turned into hours, which became a day, and at 5:27, he scanned around. Neither Rohan nor Zoey had moved; both were still stationed and locked in. He closed his eyes and rubbed his head, where a slight ache squirmed. Likely the combination of that strange dream driving a restless night and a long day. Opening his eyes, he searched for some relief in the window.

The street, brimming with motion, had only one creature that was truly stationary—a massive tree at the end of the corner. It existed in its tiny plot of earth, railed off by a small black metal fence and heavy square slabs of concrete. But even locked away in its tiny prison, it had grown mighty. It watched hundreds under its shadow, those who wandered in every direction, rushing to their destinations. From so far up, they were all so small, just pieces wandering on a chess board. And above the pedestrians, above even the tree, the skyscrapers towered.

Ian checked the time again. 5:28.

He reread what he had already studied to distract himself as more minutes spilled away. It was 6:20 when Zoey made a quiet exit and passed him without saying a word. It was 6:34 when his eyes started to hurt. Finally, it was 6:52 when Rohan stood up.

He walked over to Ian. "What are you still doing here?"

Ian shrugged. "No one told me I could go."

Rohan smiled and waved his hand in an upward motion. "I'm telling you now—let's go."

As the two walked to the elevator, Ian asked, "How long have you guys been working on Paper Now?"

"Two months."

"Two months? It seems like kind of a simple job, no?"

Rohan shook his head. "You'd be surprised. There's so many things that go into every element. You have button sizes, button position, page responsiveness, page layout, timer or no timer, customer research analytics, social media strategy, search engine optimization, so much. It's a complicated world; you need to break it down piece by piece."

"Ah, I see. Interesting," said Ian quietly.

Outside, the two waved goodbye and went in opposite directions, and, down the street, Ian made sure to stop at the tree on the corner for a second look. From the ground, it was even more impressive, a beacon that stood in contrast to the grayness of the City. Under its shadow, he saw it was transforming, a morphing green.

Its leaves hinted at orange, decorated by their decay in a

changing season. A few had already fallen off, landing dead in the soil below, while its branches shook against the cold breeze.

Despite its size, despite its might, even it can be bullied by the wind. Ian shivered.

He resumed his walk and took a deep breath, which was met with stale, smoky air that made him spit onto the concrete.

On his way home, while he sat on the train, he considered how many hours had gone into the new Paper Now. Three people. Two months. Ten hours a day. Twenty-two days a month. Three times two times ten times twenty-two. One thousand three hundred twenty hours. Fifty-five days.

Fifty-five days gone.

Ian squinted. Things were unclear, distorted. All he could make out were shades of colors—red, yellow, green. Pulling his head back, he tried to get a better look and concentrate. Then he blinked twice and saw it.

Above him were splintered pieces of stained glass, cobbled together in a confused pattern, like they had been shattered, refused, and nearly shattered again. The light they filtered came down fractured and strong, covering him and the space behind him like multicolored cobwebs.

He followed the glass and its light up toward to the roof. As he craned his neck he realized how high the ceiling went. It went up, up, up… It appeared endless, reaching toward the heavens.

Suddenly he heard a voice. "*Wait!*"

That voice. Ian turned around and tried to make sense of the scene behind him. After some effort, he made out the stranger's figure, the man who had pleaded to his mama. He was huge, but his size was disguised. He hunched with collapsed shoulders and a bent back as he held his head down and anxiously shook his leg. Ian cringed at him. An aura of slow panic hung around him like flies on dead meat.

"Don't go…" he whimpered. "Please." His voice was even weaker than before, as though every word was a pain to get out. He was choking on them.

Standing on low steps, he faced away from Ian, and instead stared down an aisle. The room was incredibly long, with a wine-red carpet stretching out toward a barely visible door at its end.

"What's going on?" asked Ian.

Another sound emerged—a continuous pitter-patter that echoed throughout the room, like someone was dragging their feet across the floor.

Ian glanced around the room. On both sides of the aisle were rows of brown benches that repeated themselves in perfect unison. Tracking the shadows that danced on them, he made out a moving smudge, deep out into the center of the room. He squinted again and realized the smudge was a distant woman, camouflaged under the rainbow light of the glass. And she was walking away.

"Please," the man whispered. "Don't go."

She was impossible to discern, obscured by the light and being so far away, but she was also impossible to miss. Her shadow was giant, stretching to the feet of the man, and she carried a mighty sound. Even as she moved away, her every step only grew louder, vibrating the space and asserting her presence. Before, her feet dragged like a quiet rhythmic roll, but now they had amplified to a steady stomp.

Again the man whispered, "Don't go."

Ian glanced back at the glass, and then at the exit beyond. Outside, the sky had turned to gray, casting the whole room into dimness. He reached into his pocket for his phone to check the time, but it wasn't there. *It must be getting late. I need to get home. That's right. I need to go home to get ready for work.*

He walked toward the man to ask him where they were. However, after a few seconds, he sensed something was wrong. He wasn't moving at all. Ian looked down—his feet were moving, his legs going up and down, but with each step forward he went nowhere, nothing changed. The man stayed the same distance away, and the woman still headed toward the exit. It seemed the whole world was moving backward, away from him, while he moved forward. Ian was stuck.

The stranger bent over and crumpled to his knees, then above him, a shadow fell. The once-high ceiling had lost its grandeur. Now it was shrinking, falling slowly onto their heads, and ahead the exit was still too far away, completely out of reach.

Terrified, Ian yelled at the man, "Sir, I need to get out of here!"

The woman was almost out of view, but her footsteps had become deafening. Every step let out the sound of steel screeching against steel, blazing across the chapel.

"Wait! Wait! I have something to say!" the stranger yelled in a final burst.

The woman turned around and yelled back: "What?"

Her voice was distorted, her tone recast, infused with the scream of steel. Her sound had become a force of nature, a wind that pushed Ian back, but he refused to yield, he refused to fall. Instead he stared deep into her faraway face. She had a faint familiarity about her, like a suspicious memory lingering somewhere between reality and fiction.

The man took a breath and paused. The light from outside had all but faded, and the room had nearly dimmed to a complete black. The woman had stopped moving, but the sound had not. It was clear as day. It was the sound of a train closing in.

The man on the ground heaved. He was sweating, dripping all over the steps. He bent his back down, all the way to the floor, too scared to stand. Finally he found his last ounce of courage and looked up to the woman. He shouted, "Don't forget your keys!"

Instantly, all became still. The far woman froze, the man stopped moving. Ian tried to take a step back, because the sound had grown painful. The blistering noise hurled tons of metal toward him, past him, and through him. It pierced his ears, overpowering everything. He turned. Was it coming from behind? No. There was nothing there but the fading light.

He looked up again. The ceiling had come so low, it appeared it would crash. Ian braced for impact, but then nothing came. It had faded away, along with the walls and the pews.

Soon there was nothing in sight except the bent man and the dark aisle leading to the exit. Then the path vanished too, and Ian was left alone with the man, both of them wrapped in a pitch black. They began to free-fall, and as they fell, the man faded away as well. Everywhere, the overwhelming sound and darkness ruled. Ian looked for his hands. They were gone. He, too, had become nothing.

The sound overpowered all his senses until it was all he could think about. It was all that there ever was, and ever would be. Light, sound, then darkness.

CHAPTER THREE

After seventeen days, Ian had successfully keyed in 137,484 customer survey data entries and learned how to dive in and out of spreadsheets, how to sew together presentations, and how to stare at websites. He had also rediscovered how long weekdays could last, and how suddenly a weekend's end could arrive.

Time accompanied by repetition had fused one day into the next, making it difficult to decipher what had passed and what was yet to come. Worsening the issue, confused visions had stirred up restless nights, which, mixed with early mornings, left him thoroughly exhausted. Thus, after he left work at 7:15 p.m. on a Thursday, he shuffled onto the subway, grabbed a silver rail, and collapsed his cheek onto it.

Around him, girls, boys, women, and men crunched together in one giant trash heap of humanity's rush hour. He embraced the suffering, squeezing himself tight in the packed train, between a middle-schooler's backpack and a morbidly obese man's belly fat, until, out of the corner of his eye, he spotted his opportunity. An old man a foot away edged toward the end of his seat. Ian took a step closer in preparation, and then the man rose.

In a split second, Ian side-stepped his way to the right, dodged a clueless passenger to his left, nudged a mother, and plopped backward onto the seat. He allowed himself to settle in, pressing himself into an awkward position, scrunched between two strangers.

Finally, he could relax. Across from him, a woman frowned, and above her hung a wide map of the subway system. He gazed at the routes' colors twisting and twirling around each other across the City, all weaved into a concord of steel. There, all in one small map, he saw endless worlds. Then he closed his eyes.

As he was carried from stop to stop, he drifted in and out of consciousness, and reality became mixed with memory and dream. His head would fall forward until his neck was strained, which shocked his eyes open, giving him a sudden wakefulness before his head began to dip again. In, out, out, in.

His mind heard the electronic voice of the conductor, the mumble of passengers, but loudest of all was the voice and its desperate cry. *Wait!* In his exhaustion, the nighttime sensations existed like a curious puzzle, slightly frightening in the moment but simultaneously exciting, enchanting. Something novel. The voice, the sky, the colors, the woman, the train, and darkness all interlocked together, forming a midnight distraction he could use to entertain himself during the day. They had already proven far more alluring to ponder than the 137,485th customer survey data entry. *What are they telling me?*

He kept drifting, until he felt the brush of someone's leg against his and awoke for a final time. He sat back and looked up.

Above him was a familiar green beanie, which covered a young woman's chestnut hair. She wore light-blue pants, a brown jacket, and rested her head against a steel rail.

Her jaw line wasn't the sharpest, and her cheeks were quite round and pudgy. Her face was imbalanced, her nose long and ears slightly too large, but that didn't matter to Ian. He barely even noticed. Instead, it was her eyes that caught his attention. They were *distracting*. While she stared into space, he became stuck in a snare; he lost himself in them. He forgot they were rolling underground in a city that housed millions, all scrambling above him. He forgot the dreams; he forgot himself. Her gaze was almost too powerful, too rich, a melted-chocolate brown that seemed otherworldly. She was beautiful.

Entering a groggy consciousness, Ian smiled and mumbled, "Hey…"

When he released the word, a bolt rippled down his electrified spine, and he jolted up. He had awoken.

He straightened himself and tried to play it off by looking straight ahead. After a moment of silence, he thought he had been successful.

"Were you talking to me?"

Ian turned to face her voice. She stared him down.

A panicked sweat leaked throughout his body. Her eyes pierced through him, and although he had the urge to look away, he couldn't.

After a one-second pause of eternity, Ian said, "Yeah."

"Oh," she said. Her voice flowed through his ears like warm water. It woke matter buried deep, stirring entombed memories. Their movement exhumed hidden emotions, dragging them to the surface of his mind. Joy, worry, and regret all spun around each other before rapidly coalescing into one solid uncertainty.

She stared at him, as if expecting a follow-up, but Ian offered none. After the standoff, she raised her head up to face the car, away from him, and closed her eyes.

Ian resumed looking straight ahead, but now his body had tensed. He had contorted his feet across each other and locked his arms by his sides. He maintained this pose until the conductor announced that his stop would be next. He took a breath and realized it was now or never. He turned to her and saw that she had turned around to face the exit, preparing for an escape.

She'll probably get off at the next stop, and if she gets off at the stop, and I get off at my stop, she'll think I'm following her, and that won't be good because I don't want her to think that I am following her, but perhaps she might not think that, but perhaps she would, and that would certainly be bad. He needed to say something now.

"So what's your name?" huffed out Ian.

This time she didn't turn her head at all and instead spoke to the open air, "Are you still talking to me?"

"Yeah."

"It's Hallie," she said. Again, Hallie looked at Ian.

"What's yours?"

"Ian."

Hallie paused before saying, "Ian's a good name."

He raced through his mind, looking for a smooth follow-up. He needed to find something to say, something suave, anything at all. Eventually, a meek response bubbled to the surface. "I like your hat."

For a split second, Hallie gave up the tiniest half smile, then she returned to a flat expression. It was enough. Her warmth hit him immediately. His shoulders dropped, his arms eased, and he smiled. Trapped in the underground, pulled along by the subway, there was an escape.

"Thanks," Hallie said. "I really like it too."

She took it off and let her hair fall out beside her. Rubbing her fingers across the hat, she said, "I actually made it myself."

"That's cool."

She held it out. "Check it."

"Oh, sure," Ian said uncertainly as he touched the fabric. It wasn't smooth, with plenty of uneven holes, but it was soft and vibrant. Its bright green stood out against the dark hues of the underground car, offering some life in a gloom starving for it.

"It's nice, very nice. Very soft."

"*Approaching 40th and 8th Avenue.*"

The sound of the conductor cut through the moment, and Ian remembered why he was talking to her in the first place. He handed back the hat and hurriedly pushed himself up from his seat. "Oh, I need to go, this is my stop."

"Me too," she said.

They stood silently next to one another until the doors opened, and they were thrust into a crowd eagerly waiting to get on. As they walked out, Ian went right and she went left. He stopped and turned and watched her walk away. She waved. "See you later. Maybe."

He hesitated, trying to decide what to say, but then she became too far away to hear him. As she disappeared into the City, a raw blend of joy spiked with regret flowed throughout his body. He regretted not talking to her more, but he rejoiced that he had met her. Seeing her among the crowd, she held a certain grace, a glow that cut through the dark of the underground. The girl with the green beanie and leather jacket. Feeling the friction of his collar against his neck, Ian wondered what she had been doing all day.

L ost in a trance, Ian gazed beyond the horizon, searching for clarity, but he found only a hazy blue. With dim sight and heavy breaths, he glanced around, fearing he would be lost forever. He spun his head, but all around him was purely the suffocating blue.

He closed his eyes, an attempt to escape the overbearing blue through the dark. He could think in the dark. He took slow, careful breaths, in and out. In and out. *All that was is all there will be.* Gingerly, he touched his stomach, felt his soft flesh, and confirmed: he was.

He opened his eyes, blinked twice, and everything was clear. He was floating, and below him, calm blue waves folded into each other, crashing and fading away into the sea, only to constantly be reborn as another.

To the east, the water glittered like flickering stars as the sun's reflection upon them appeared then disappeared then appeared again with every crest then trough then crest again. To the west, the waves stayed clear and simply crawled and tussled together. And above him, a blue sky, empty of clouds, reigned.

"How long will it take to get back?"

The sea's rhythm was his only response. He blinked again and focused. *Think: What is out there? Is there a boat? Is someone there who can take me home?*

No, none of that mattered. The real question was: *How did I get here?*

Ian thought back to work, to Hallie, lights, colors, *Wait!*, exhaustion, the darkness… He was dreaming.

Yes, Ian decided. He was dreaming. The thought calmed him, but he still yearned to know where he was.

After scanning around, he spotted something in the distance, something no bigger than a tiny dot. He tried to take a step forward but made no progress. The dot remained so far away.

"This again?" Ian tilted his head toward the sea, clenched his fists, and punched them into the air. Then he closed his eyes and lunged forward.

He felt a mild breeze twirl around him, and when he opened his eyes, he had stopped but had progressed forward. He saw it was no dot, but a boat, and sitting on the edge of the boat was a woman.

He paused and squinted. She looked familiar. Curly hair… silly face… *Lizzy.*

Lizzy. Ian was certain, but she was *different*. Her hair was shorter, and her face was a touch younger and it held an uncertain expression. Curious, Ian studied her. He had never seen her like that before. She looked… *worried*.

She leaned on the small rowboat's prow with her legs dipped into the ocean and her hands clasped together while she stared at the horizon.

"Lizzy," asked Ian as he floated in the sky above her, "what are you doing here?"

He received nothing but her silence and the flow of waves.

"We need to go," he shouted down at her. "We need to go home."

She didn't look up; she didn't acknowledge him. Instead, she opened a hand and revealed a pebble, a smooth oval stone in one of her palms.

"What is that?"

She said nothing. Instead, the stone began to slowly expand.

Ian peered down, mesmerized. It grew in all dimensions, and soon it was large enough that she was forced to hold it firmly with both hands. It had gone from barely a thing at all to something undeniably real.

He leaned in to get a better view of the stone, but it quickly became easy to see, even at his distance. It flourished.

The stone ballooned to the size of a pillow, and Lizzy leaned back. Ian saw it weighed on her; it seemed to take all her strength to simply hold it in her arms.

"Lizzy, what are you doing?"

The boat rocked. The stone's rapid maturation now forced Lizzy to cradle it against the boat and her body, support it between her legs and stomach.

"Lizzy," cried Ian, "let it go!"

She did not. As the stone became a boulder, it pushed the boat down. With the boat tipped forward, she started to slip off and dip further into the ocean, still clutching the stone. Limb by limb, she became submerged, until all that remained above water were tired eyes and her short curly hair. And then she was gone.

"Lizzy!" Ian froze as her head fell beneath the waves and he could no longer make her out. He desperately searched the ocean, looking for any trace of her, but he found nothing. Moments later, the boulder resurfaced, growing no more. Instead it floated calmly along the waves and drifted away with the tide. Then the light on the sea dimmed.

He looked up. The sun had faded, and blue had turned to black, with no stars shining through. The ocean below too had become darkness; its black waves thrashed in an empty universe.

Gravity pulled on Ian's stomach and turned it over. For the first time, as he free-fell, he sensed his weight in its entirety: a thick and useless lump that only dragged him down.

He whipped his arms against the air, but it was no use. He was falling, falling into the empty ocean. He hit the waves, fell deeper, and its emptiness engulfed his lungs while a train's low scream filled his ears.

CHAPTER FOUR

Zoey shoved her finger past Ian's face, toward his screen. "That one."

He moved the mouse and hovered over the pastel brown. She jotted down the color's hex number: #836953.

8-3-6-9-5-3. How strange that an entire color could be represented in six digits.

Rohan, who sat next to him, brushed against him to get a better look at the screen. "Do you think they'll want the color to be the same as what they had before? They're paying us for a redesign."

Ian stared straight ahead, crushed in by their two bodies. The ordeal had begun when he asked, "What color should the button be?"

"I would think so," Zoey said. "There's still some brand equity. You don't want to confuse the customer."

Rohan leaned in. "Let me drive for a second, Ian."

Ian lifted his hand off the keyboard and rolled backward. Rohan drooped himself over Ian, trapping him in a lock with Rohan in front and Zoey behind before he proceeded to hover over every color imaginable, flicking from red to green to white, updating the center of the screen with a never-ending world of options. By Ian's count, they had looked at least twelve.

"Try brown again," Zoey said.

So Rohan did. Then he went back to other colors.

Ian checked the time in the corner of the screen. 4:55 p.m.

"Give me a second," Rohan said. He stood up and walked to his computer.

Zoey jumped in, pushing Ian, and resumed with the button. He sighed and watched the colors transform. She flicked from red to yellow to green to brown. They seemed so flat on the screen. Green to yellow to red. Exhaustion had taken its toll, and the colors weren't helping. Brown to gray to red once again. His concentration waned, his eyes' focus took on a delay. Red to yellow to brown. The colors did not glow like they had in dream.

"What are you guys working on?" Ian twisted his chair and saw Oscar approaching.

"We're trying to decide on Paper Now's color scheme," Zoey said.

"Ah," Oscar said. He came over and filled the spot Rohan had occupied and scrunched over Ian. "Did you guys consider something modern? Maybe silver, maybe gray, something with a nice bezel?"

Zoey shook her head. "My concern is that we'll confuse the customer. Their old scheme was all brown."

Then Rohan rolled over with his computer on his lap. "I did some research, and apparently red leads to more conversions. It ignites more emotion."

"Interesting," Oscar said.

Ian watched Zoey begin to flick the mouse with greater velocity and aggression. She snapped it over and back, dissatisfied with every option.

"Well, I got to go," Oscar said. "Dinnertime."

Rohan and Zoey gave their goodbyes, while Ian stayed silent and trapped.

Zoey resumed the argument. "I just don't know if we should be making such a big decision this quick."

"Fine," Rohan said flatly. "Let's call them."

"Okay, okay," Zoey said. She pulled out her cellphone, tapped in a number, turned on the speaker, and the three of them waited.

"Hi, is this Jack? This is Zoey from Modern Solutions. We're trying to sort out an issue and wanted your guys' input."

They received a grunt in return.

"Yes, so we were wondering what color you wanted for your color scheme. We're trying to decide between a gray, red, and the old color, brown."

"*Give me a second*," the voice buzzed.

They waited, and Ian looked up at Zoey and Rohan, then the time. 5:10.

"Sorry about that. What were we talking about again?"

"The color," Zoey said. "We wanted to know what color scheme you guys wanted."

"Oh. Let me check with our marketing people."

"Okay, do you want us to call you ba—" They were put on hold.

Rohan grinned and stretched his arms over his head. "I'm telling you guys, red would be killer." Meanwhile, Zoey tapped the table with her fingers.

The phone snapped back. "Hello? Hello?"

Zoey jumped on it. "Yeah, we're here."

"Okay. James said just do whatever looks good. Your pick."

Zoey sighed. "All right, you got it. Bye." Then the line went dead.

She straightened herself and let out something between a sigh and a yell. "Look, I don't want to make the decision for us, but we need to move on, so let's decide on something."

Rohan pointed at the screen. "Red looks real good. We can just ship them our proposal and see what they think."

The two went back and forth, forth and back. They circled around their arguments, all the while growing louder and louder. Their voices turned into some kind of rhythmic shrill, coming and going in a perfect painful harmony. Ian rubbed his scalp; between them and the glare of the screen, his head throbbed. He glanced at the time again. 5:30.

"You've been awfully quiet."

Ian's gaze snapped up. Zoey and Rohan stared at him.

"What do you think?" Zoey asked.

"Uh, I really don't know. You all have valid points."

Zoey crossed her arms and leaned against the table. "You'll be our tiebreaker."

A tingle spread from Ian's hands, went up his arms, journeyed through his shoulders, and emerged in his mouth. Frustration had simmered into steam, and in a brief moment of release, he let it out.

"I think anything could work. Look, we've spent too much time on this. It isn't going to break or make anything. Stop worrying so much. No one will care that much about the color. It really doesn't matter."

A fat silence fell over them. The air in the room had thinned, become choking, suffocating. A passing terror fluttered across Ian's chest. Rohan looked slightly down, while Zoey glared at him, a mix of disappointment combined with aggravation.

Clumsily, more of Ian's words spilled out. "That said, it's all really good ideas. Great research and thinking. Probably... red. Red makes a lot of sense. Rohan made a great point about the research, and I think we could make it look really good."

After that, more silence ensued until Zoey concluded, "Fine. Have it your way. We'll make it red."

There was a tacit agreement, and it was done.

The team remained quiet for the rest of the day as they worked separately in silence. Ian's guts whispered to him to say something while the knot in his stomach slowly unwound, but he refused to listen.

6:25 p.m.

Ian rose, prepared to leave. He scanned the office and realized it had changed compared to when he had first arrived. The glass windows revealing the City were hazy in the late fall, projecting only neon and weak streetlights in the afternoon. The walls seemed tighter, pulling the room into a box. The black monitors lining the floorspace were darker than ever. It was all so flat, uninspiring, and in a way he did not understand, unsettling.

He realized his back was bent over, so he forced himself to stand up straight.

As he entered the elevator, he joined a suited man who stood in the corner. He was bald with a thick double chin and clutched a black briefcase with a grubby hand. Ian tried to turn toward the wall to look away, but there was something about the man that captivated him. He couldn't help but stare at the way tiny little beads of sweat dripped down his forehead, or how his thick stomach rumbled with every breath, or how his engorged nose, red and stiff, looked to be choking on itself.

Ian realized his back had bent over again.

The man smiled and nodded at him. "Ready for the weekend?"

Ian, caught off guard, turned away from the man and faced the elevator door. "Yes, it'll be great."

Staring at the man's reflection in the door of the elevator, he saw weariness in his eyes. Ian yawned; he yearned for sleep, for dream.

THE LIGHT from the display kept Ian's eyes burning on a slow roast and his mind awake. He had been scrolling, searching through the night. Sleep had called on him more than once, but he refused to listen. Each time he put his phone down, the small black portal summoned him back without much struggle.

He scanned through pictures and videos of friends and strangers, each one a captured memory, a twinkle in time, and consumed them ravenously. He gave them a single glance, sucked in their frail vitality, and scrolled on. He saw great sights: an acquaintance climbing an impossible mountain, a forgotten friend healing the sick, and countless suns, all from his bed.

Earlier, in the midst of his digital travels, a notification had popped up on his screen.

I'm in the city tomorrow. You free?

Ian gave it a glance, considered his options, and pushed it out of view.

He journeyed endlessly, continuously, always finding himself looped back to the beginning, only to repeat the process once more. He kept scrolling, scrolling, scrolling. That night, nothing else mattered except the intravenous drip of data directly feeding his brain. But deep into the late hours of the night, something stopped him.

Ian took his finger off the screen and stared. His pupils dilated. His hand took on an imperceptible tremble.

On his screen was a picture of Lizzy. She smiled a wide grin and flashed her hand to the camera. Around her fourth finger was a silver band with a glowing stone on top. Her new diamond ring.

Just engaged!!! said her caption.

Ian stared at the two words and decided to send her a message. He opened up her contact and quickly wrote: *Congrats on the engagement.*

Then he paused before he returned to scrolling.

She only took thirty seconds to respond.

Thanks! Stay tuned—family bridal shower coming soon!

Immediately he responded: *When's the wedding???*

January 2nd ;)!

Ian double-checked the current date. It was October 16th.

After rereading the message one last time, he turned off his phone, threw it aside, and squirmed around in his bed, searching for comfort while he stared at the ceiling.

Lizzy, the wild, annoying cousin with the puffy hair, was getting married. He chuckled. Anything could happen, he supposed. Maybe he would even get to see Hallie again.

Ian closed his eyes, and his thoughts carried him along a path of memories and dreams, tainted by both lights and shadows, until it all ended when weariness won.

I an waited on the edge of the roundabout, a concrete circle with a white border and curved arrows pointing around. The intersection encircled a dirt mound, where massive oaks stood tall. They spread their branches out wide into the sky, stretching bright-green leaves that flittered slowly.

Sitting on grass beside the road, Ian watched the traffic move, or at least try to move. There was a jam: two city buses, with their occupants hidden inside behind dark windows, were stuck around several cars. He cupped his ear toward the mess. Their engines sounded so faint, as if lost in the far-off distance, while the whir of an ambulance siren played somewhere ever farther.

The ambulance murmured *"Eeee-oooo, eeee-oooo"* until its cry dissipated away entirely.

Ian examined the cars with curiosity, as shadows from the oaks' leaves danced above them. They moved at a glacial pace, a few inches there, a few inches here, until, after about ten minutes, Ian realized that the first bus had returned. It had finished a loop and arrived back at its starting point.

He rose from the grass and said, "Time to go." Then he

glanced around. Beyond the horizon, outside of the round-about, were simple plains in all directions, unkempt grasslands which grew tall and tangled in one great open heap. Ian decided he would mow them later, not today.

He started walking around the circle. It took a while, but he was in no rush, and by the time he reached the opposite side of the roundabout, he counted the bus had passed him seven times. There he found the traffic circle's sole entrance and exit: a single straight road that jutted out and went far into the distance, with an end beyond his vision. He journeyed onto the road and approached its sole inhabitant, an old woman who sat behind a small black desk in the middle of the road, blocking the entrance to the roundabout.

Her hair was frazzled and gray, and intersecting wrinkles flooded her face, spreading throughout her cheeks and down onto her neck. Ancient and withered, she could barely look up, with eyes dragged down by drooping flesh.

Ian approached her while she stared blankly at the road in front of her. He saw that her skin, presumably once a more vibrant brown, had grown pale and sickly.

"Excuse me," said Ian, "where are we?"

She did not respond but instead moaned under her breath. "*Huhveei, huhhvi.*"

He couldn't understand her. She had a thick Spanish accent, and her words were slurred, almost lazily released. Her voice was nasally; it seemed like she wasn't getting enough air.

"What's that?" asked Ian.

More mumbling. "*Huhevi, huvve.*"

He shook his head and instead followed her line of sight. Looking down the road, he realized a red sedan had arrived and was waiting in front of the woman's desk.

The old woman stared blankly into the car's window and continued to moan on, while the car in front of her inched forward before stopping closer to the desk. Meanwhile, Ian heard more honks originating from somewhere far away.

"Excuse me!" he yelled at the car. "I need to know where you're going."

He received no response but the old woman's mumbles and the quiet hum of distant cars.

Ian stepped toward the car to demand the driver tell him where they were. Peeking inside, he saw the driver clear under the daylight. Lizzy.

Lizzy? He stared at her, it was Lizzy, but she was *different*. She had short, controlled hair and an uncertain expression. Examining her through the glass, he thought he had never before seen her like that—worried.

Wait.

He stumbled back a step and ran his hand through his hair. *That's not right.* He had seen her like this before. Where?

Yes. She had been worried in the boat. She had been worried while holding the growing stone, while the sea tugged on her. And he had seen her worried somewhere else; he was certain. He mulled on it, and then it came to him.

It had been her. Under the colored glass. She had been the woman walking away, down the aisle, the woman with the metal steps, the woman who made the stranger with the proud voice so afraid.

The old woman continued to look ahead into the car, weakly shaking her fist and indiscriminately muttering.

"Lizzy!" he shouted to the car.

Lizzy said nothing. She rested her hand against her face and waited for the traffic to move.

"*Avieii, Ahveee.*"

Frustrated, Ian turned, slapped the desk, and shouted at the woman, "What are you babbling about?"

"*Jhaavi, Jaahvii,*" she said.

Ian leaned against the table and stewed, wondering what to

do. Lizzy appeared stuck, and the woman would not stop buzzing in his ear. He nearly wanted to wake up. Then, finally, something interesting appeared in the horizon. Out in the grasslands, outside the roundabout, something budded.

First, in the far distance, small ones flourished, rising up like simple gray metal rectangles. Then, without hesitation, they proliferated.

They emerged faster and faster and burgeoned closer and closer to Ian and to the roundabout. Out of the earth, bigger and grander designs hatched. Each one was a building complete with windows and terraces, arches and high doors. They sprouted from the ground, stretched toward the sky, and towered in the distance.

Ian watched their progress in awe. They germinated at a breathtaking pace, multiplying throughout the plains until the greatest structures bloomed. They reached an apex on the edge of the roundabout, their vertical growth unmatched. They all were giants of glass and steel, twinkling under the sunlight. They stood at impossible heights, with unseen tops cutting into the sky, a grandeur beyond anything Ian had ever seen. True skyscrapers.

He leaned back, searching for a glimpse of their crowns and failing.

"Incredible."

Standing above them, the urban landscape stared back down onto the buses, the oaks, the roundabout, the woman, the sedan, and Ian. It cast its shadows over them, covering them in a calm shade. And as the development finished, the cars within the roundabout began to pick up their pace.

The old woman moaned again, and Lizzy drove her car around the desk to join the roundabout. *What is happening?* Behind the car, deep in the horizon, Ian could see something growing dark.

In the center of the roundabout, the oaks continued to

sway, now hidden under the towers' shadows. *They will starve for light*, he thought. They would be forced to survive off crumbs dripped in from solar noons. When he looked to the colossuses that hung above them, there was no question. They paled against the ambition of the skyscraper.

Traffic continued to accelerate, and the sound of a train emerged, emanating from somewhere off in the horizon. Ian listened for it and prepared for its impact.

In front of him, the old woman mumbled one last "*Javi?*" before she dissipated into the air.

Above him, the sky grew dark, and lights from the newly formed city grew dim. Ian, feeling the fatigue of his body, sat down to gaze at the fading megalopolis. He whispered, "Good night."

The last light of the towers went black, followed by the cars, the landscape, the city, until even the forgotten oaks ceased moving. They were all swallowed by a warm darkness that embraced him, embraced them all. He welcomed the fall as gravity pulled him down.

The last thing he heard was the growing train approaching, and the last image he saw was the red car finishing its final loop around the roundabout. Then nothing.

CHAPTER FIVE

A s Friday waned, Ian waited. He was looking for someone
on his team, anyone, to leave before him. Every day, he
had progressively departed earlier during the eternity that
composed last week, so another early exit was not an option.

After taking his seventh water break of the day, he sat in
front of his computer and stared at the same spreadsheet he
had been looking at for the last hour. Progress had ceased; he
had become lost in its cells. Disorientation had peaked a half
an hour ago when he discovered all the work he had done was
completely wrong, utterly incorrect. He had blinked twice,
shook his head, and stared at it, but did nothing. Now he was
on burnout. In this weary, unfocused state, he managed to hear
what he had been tuning out before: the lights sang an infuri-
ating low buzz, coworkers spoke of a printer out of paper, and
outside, cars honked, strangers passed by, and a stray bird
chirped. He opted for the window.

The tree on the corner of the street, contained in its tiny
plot of earth, had lost nearly all its leaves, and the few that
remained had curled and browned, prepared to leave. Its
branches shook and shivered while pedestrians hustled along in

coats and hats. The towering skyscrapers happily shoveled in wind and hurled it on them all, throwing it down onto the block at violent velocities. The air was becoming crisp. The sky gray. The days short. Winter had arrived.

Ian's focus drifted while his eyes floated over the outside world. Soon his mind ended up nowhere in particular at all, simply stuck trying to catch pestering thoughts as they dashed around.

First the voice. "Okay, Mama."
Then Lizzy in the church. "What!"
Followed by the stone.
And lastly, the roundabout. "Javi."
And again the voice. "Okay, Mama…"

"See you later," she said. Ian spun in his chair and saw Zoey waving goodbye. He waved, looked at the screen for two more minutes, then rose.

The moment he stepped outside, the City's wind stung him like a blade. It cut into the side of his face, and as he tried to walk, it pushed him back.

He needed to move.

Ian breathed in the frosty air and began to jog, then run. He rushed down the block, snapping his leather shoes against the concrete pavement, trying to forget the cold and push his mind toward anything else: What he had done yesterday, what he did today, what he would need to do tomorrow. Anything was more interesting than that wind. He needed to forget to move and to move to forget. That is, until he saw an exit.

At the end of the street rested an ominous entrance to a dark and dirty subway passage. He hustled down its gum-stained stairs and entered its graffitied tunnels, becoming one with the crowd, which shuffled in and out. With every step, his muscles loosened and his mind eased. In recent days, the descent into subway stations had become joyous occasions.

Down in the dungeon, heat was trapped and offered imminent relief.

Even farther down, down below the gray sky, down beneath the skyscrapers, down underneath the earth, down on the train platform, heat soaked deeper into his body. It filled every inch of his cranium, until, for the first time that week, he thought of nothing. Not work or dreams or past or future. Instead he only scanned the other pedestrians. To his immediate left, an old woman gazed into space; to his near right, a young man stared at his phone. And spread across the platform were countless others who stood next to him, all swirling in their own thoughts. They all waited together and they all waited alone for the next train.

An uncomfortable stillness rumbled in Ian's body.

Relief arrived in the form of metal screeching against metal. It was birthed as a whisper but quickly grew into a shout. It was his train, coming to carry him off. And as the sound grew louder, so, too, did memories of the dreams. They returned suddenly, like the wind cutting into his face.

He saw the old woman moaning by the rising city.

"*Doors opening.*"

He spotted Lizzy going under, dragged down by the stone.

"*Doors closing.*"

He squinted at the lights of the church.

"*Next stop is: 40th Street.*"

And he heard the stranger's voice boom through his consciousness.

Leaning into his seat, Ian closed his eyes and let his head hang while the train carried him home. He maintained this posture until he sensed a presence hanging above him. With reluctance, he pulled his eyes open and peeked across the car. There, in the train's curved glass, he saw the reflection of a woman standing above him. Her image was difficult to decipher, blurred and dimmed in the black backdrop of the underground, but he still knew it must be her.

Hallie.

His heart ticked faster, which angered him. He considered his options and decided there was only one possibility. While he raised his head, he tried to not make it obvious, but her eyes dragged him in. He stared at her, and she turned to face him. Then he quickly turned to face straight ahead.

Ian touched the back of his neck. A thin layer of sticky, slimy sweat glazed his skin.

"Were you looking at me?"

Ian snapped his neck up. "What?"

"I said, 'Why were you staring at me?'"

"I wasn't. And that's not what you said."

Hallie mockingly nodded her head. "Okay. Yeah, all right. Good to see you too, Ian."

Her eyes made it far too easy to become lost. Within milliseconds, his brain sent him to a quagmire where it was impossible to tell up from down and left from right. But the way she looked back told him what he wanted to know. He knew it was time, time for a leap.

As Ian spoke, his words didn't feel right, with each syllable barely able to land before the next, all falling down like slippery dominoes. Fortunately for him, they still exited in a way that made sense.

"You want to get lunch?"

Hallie stared at him, finally a little uncertain. She studied him before she offered a shallow scoff. "I don't think a subway relationship will work out."

He let out an involuntarily stupid squeaky snort-laugh. "Do they come up often?"

She frowned. "No, but everybody here's a stranger. Or just strange." She looked down at him and asked, "Why should we get lunch?"

Ian looked down at his feet and paused to think about the question. He didn't have a good answer. So he looked up at her and shrugged. "Why not?"

She thought about it, then nodded. "Fair point." She pulled out her phone and thrust it in front of his face. "Here."

He tapped in his number, handed it back, and again looked up at her. "So, are you from here?"

She shook her head. "No, I moved here about five years ago... but I don't think I'll ever leave."

"Oh?"

"I went to school here."

"Where were you from before?"

"A small town... It doesn't really matter. I need to go, this is my stop."

Ian turned to the window, and sure enough, it was the stop.

She waved. "See you later."

He watched her walk out the door and disappear from view. Soon the space where she had stood was filled by new bodies, and once again, he was left riding the train alone.

As the car accelerated, he regained his breath, and his heartbeat returned to normal. He quickly realized that he had missed his stop, but that didn't matter. The excitement that he had buried was now too alluring to resist. It had covertly crawled back to full force and now emerged proudly as an undeniable glow dawned in his chest. He smiled, he grinned.

He would see her again.

No stars shined outside. They were all shrouded behind the City's aura as it spilled its polluted glow into the night, all over those distant stars. Embraced by this artificial light, in one small room, in one small building, in one small world, Ian lay in bed awaiting sleep. It had evaded him for the last hour, for his thoughts had proven far too busy. They ran in circles, chasing one another by the tail in an eager fever.

Hallie, Brown, Red, Yellow, Green, Voice, Glass, Train, Stone, City, Darkness, Dream. Hallie, Brown…

Ian ripped his eyes open and went to the kitchen. He grabbed a cup and filled it with tap water. He sat on a lonely chair, his only chair, and gazed out his window. There were a few scattered individuals, but now, so late into the night, the streets were mostly empty. Yet even in this sleepy state, the City made certain all its residents knew it was still alive. It still glared. All of its lights—its streetlights, traffic signs, neon banners, apartment lamps—cut through the darkness. Sounds from hidden, faraway streets rumbled, called, screamed for action. Smoke and dust particles lingered in every scent on every block. Nameless cars, nameless people, moved in a constant frenzy.

He soaked it all in, trying to calm the sea of his mind, but the sight failed to bring him peace. Staring into the illuminated dark, he could only think of the sprouting city from his dream, its glimmer, its glory. Seeing it here, awake, was different.

The City was *impressive*, he admitted. Man had bent earth to its whim. Every block presented a strong fusion of steel, cement, brick, and glass, designed to last, silently screaming to all its serfs: *I am King*.

But was it beautiful? Ian decided *no*. Not really. The glare before him was nothing compared to the glow of his dreams. Awake, the lights held a harshness and an artificial tenor, which was all he could notice. On the other hand, the dreams had been beautiful glimpses of something new, a promise of something fantastic.

Ian took in a final gulp of water and put the cup down. Then he crawled back into bed and pulled his blankets over himself. Cradled in their warmth, he yearned for the strange dreams, where everything was different and unknown. He yearned to understand them, to understand why they had come to him. He had considered writing them down but decided it was unnecessary. When he was a boy, he would forget nearly all his dreams, but now it seemed times had changed. Recently, they had become so vivid and so rich, he could remember every detail with perfect clarity.

Ian glanced around the apartment. He thought he had visited the room before, but perhaps not. The floor was spotless: no blemishes, no dirt, no dust. It shined so brightly that it convinced him to bend down to see if it would catch his reflection, but it did not. As he walked around the space, he felt odd, like a vague memory whispered to him at too low of a volume to hear it.

At first it appeared the lone decoration in the room was a plastic-wrapped couch, neatly placed against the wall, which was so perfectly smooth and white and barren that it, in its own way, was a marvel. Ian approached the couch to sit, but then he spotted something that stole his attention.

It was a painting. No, it was *the* painting. It dominated the room, standing high and wide against the back wall. It hung far above the couch, an oil painting of a dark-blue riverbank. The river, flowing next to a dry grassland, reflected the light of a starry night in its dark waters.

As he approached it, he felt the wind's drift and the smoothness of soft rocks by the bank. He could see the water's purity, hear it flow. How had he not noticed it before? He was right there, right there by the bank, and he could breathe in—

"*No puedo… No puedo… OLVIDÉ!*"

The painting vanished and the scream froze his heart.

He had never heard anything like it before, but understood it instantly. It was visceral, primordial, like an animal howling as blood drips from their chest, or a lover seeing their love drop dead. *Panic.*

Ian moved, and the floor began to rumble. A force of gravity tugged at his legs, but he fought it. He broke through, propelled himself forward, and ran into the next room, the kitchen. There, standing around a wooden table, were two women.

Ian immediately recognized one of them: the old woman, the woman from the road, the weary mumbling lady. She stood in a floral dress and shivered with her head face down, toward her feet.

Across from her was another woman, but Ian did not recognize her. She was white, younger, Ian guessed in her late thirties, with blonde hair and a thin figure. Her face had a sheen, the product of a measured combination of tanning lotions and sun booths. Thick mascara and dark eyeliner camouflaged her face, but Ian saw more, he saw beyond it all. He saw grayness, weariness under her synthetic shine. He saw sunken and emaciated cheeks.

It was her eyes that stood out. Her irises, a deep piercing blue, could have been inviting under the eyeliner, yet Ian recoiled when he stared at her deeper. The whites of her eyes held another hue. They were bloodshot.

The floor's tilt accelerated at an increasing pace, going up and down and back and forth. The old woman twisted her neck up and stared down the younger blonde woman. "No!" the old woman screamed. "*¡Déjame en paz!* Go away! Away!"

Tears began to flow, and she muffled out, "*Donde esta…
Donde esta… Donde esta,* Javi?"

She wandered back and forth, as if searching around the
room, while she lightly touched the sides of her face. In the
process, the shaking eased, and Ian regained his footing.

The young woman said nothing, she only stared forward.
Her disturbing gaze met Ian's eyes, but when he moved out of
the way, she kept looking straight. After a spell of silence, the
old woman's tears softened, and the floor stilled.

"What is happening?" asked Ian.

Then the young woman vanished, completely gone. Out of
a reflexive shock, Ian walked several steps back, but barely a
moment later, she reappeared and materialized right in front
of him and next to the old woman. He flinched at her appear-
ance, stumbled back, tripped on his feet, and fell to the floor.
The blonde grabbed the old woman by the shoulder and
squeezed into her flesh. "Adriana," she said. "You do
remember."

The old woman mumbled and shivered. She looked at the
blonde woman with wide eyes in pure terror. Her lip quivered.
She cried out, "No!"

When the word finished leaving Adriana's mouth, it seemed
to Ian that all things had been imperceptibly paused. Something
was *wrong*, fundamentally wrong, like his muscles knew things
had changed, but his brain needed a little more time to process
the update. His muscles knew the truth first: the laws of physics
had been rewritten within a millionth of a second, tuned to the
chords of emotion, and nothing would ever be the same.

Everything erupted.

The floor thrashed. An unstoppable earthquake ripped
through the ground beneath them. The floorboards under Ian
split into pieces. Planks cracked and shoved against one
another, launching endless splinters into the air. They collided

with his face and rolled across his cheeks, but he felt no pain. Instead they arrived warm and wet. Swiftly, he lost all footing and found himself at the mercy of the calamity.

Simultaneously, the blonde woman's face transformed. In rapid succession, it became featureless, with her first losing her eyes, then her nose, and finally her mouth, before she disappeared entirely, forgotten from existence.

Meanwhile, in the middle of the room, Adriana seemed lost in her panic. She shuddered, fell back onto a shaking seat, and clutched herself, while the walls around her joined in with the eruption and rolled like the waves of a tsunami.

Ian tried to get up but slipped again. As he fell, his leg became jammed in an open crack in the floorboards. He looked down and saw within the exposed hole a great darkness, nothing but a void. He tried to ignore it and crawl out of the cavity, but immediately another plank, one below his left hand, cracked. It gave way and trapped his arm inside. The space around his leg collapsed inward and swallowed the wood around it like a whirlpool, dragging him down with it.

His grip loosened while he continued to thrash with the shaking of the room. He gasped for air as his lungs struggled to function amid his panic. It was all too much. The deepest pit of his stomach had summoned an overwhelming dread, like a tumor had settled within and expanded to fill all available space, squeezing tight inside of his body.

Ian summoned all the air he had left inside of him to let out a final, hollow scream. "Help me!"

In response, he received only Adriana's labored breathing and the faint metallic screech of a train in the distance as he fell, and darkness surrounded him.

CHAPTER SIX

Ian woke on Saturday morning, shivering. He rolled over and checked the time: 9:17 a.m.

After he rose, he approached his window. Each step was difficult. The layer of sweat that had accumulated across his body during the night tugged on him. Some of it was still flowing, inching toward his feet, there to serve as a constant reminder of what had happened.

He pushed the glass open, and a crisp breeze rolled in. Outside of his tiny apartment, he could see the metamorphosis of sidewalk trees had reached total completion. Each had gone barren as stripped leaves rested dead beside brittle trunks.

In the brief stillness, he could hear a scream. He shivered. Then he closed the window.

He stumbled into the bathroom and pulled off his boxers. He dipped into the shower and turned the faucet to cold, hard water. While he stood, he pressed his hands against the wall, letting the water fall onto his back, trying to breathe slowly, trying to refocus. His mind was stuck on what it could see so clearly: the painting, the panic, the collapse.

He rubbed his foot against the shower floor's tiles. He

needed to ensure they were real, to validate their solidity. Since he had awoken, the floor had remained uneasy.

After he shivered again, he turned down the faucet and let warm water flow.

The voice.

Lizzy.

The old woman. No, Ian realized. *Adriana.*

The blonde.

And Javi.

He shuffled through his memories, searching for any trace of the voice, Adriana, or the blonde. And who was Javi? He plunged down deeper, mentally traveling as far back as he could, back to when he could barely think, trying to remember, but he found nothing. Perhaps he had forgotten. Maybe misheard.

The dreams had begun as interesting novelties, new adventures that he breathed in during the night and could breathe out by morning. Now they stuck. They had evolved. They crept, sneaking into his slumber, and penetrated his thoughts throughout the day.

The flare. The church. The rock. The roundabout. The collapse. Darkness.

They were no longer ethereal suggestions. They had thickened, grown heavy, and in some ways, more comfortable. In truth, he admitted, despite their occasional terrors, Lizzy drowning beneath the waves and Adriana's panic, he found himself strangely enjoying them.

Some had conjured exhilarating images: a flaring sky, a blossoming city. Even the frightening ones enthralled him. They had clutched his chest and injected him with hysteria, and that was a part of their *charm*. He knew that the nightmare from last night would follow him into day, linger in his brain, and hypnotize him. He had not been that close to an open heart in months, maybe even years. Last night, he had received a small taste of true agony, true torment, and it helped him feel alive. They all helped him feel alive.

Under the warm water, he wanted to search. He wanted to find their truth, to search for their secrets, to understand what they were trying to tell him.

But Ian also knew it wouldn't be a morning for searching. It was time to go. He had a place to be.

When Ian pressed the golden doorbell, it gave him the greatest satisfaction he had experienced in weeks: a tactile, solid click.

He waited in front of the gray metal slab, a door marked 9B, which secured its contents like a vault. Having once again ignored his intuition, he found himself outside Lizzy's boyfriend's apartment.

No, that's not right. It had probably become more Lizzy's apartment now, after all.

He watched the door vibrate ever so slightly as muffled music from inside tried to escape. He moved to press the doorbell again, but then the knob turned.

Lizzy cracked the door open and gave a glowing smile. "I'm so glad you made it!"

The music, a pointed pop, melted waves out of the gap, leaking synthesized life into the hallway. Lizzy, covered in a thick sweater, held the door open halfway, using a bare foot with toenails highlighted by painted sparkles. She twisted her neck behind her and yelled, "Give me a second!"

He stepped forward and snuck through the door. "It's good to see you again, Lizzy."

Leading him inside, she said, "I want you to meet everybody, especially Regi. My mom's here too! She wanted to talk to you."

Passing room by room, he spotted a clutter of unfamiliar

family and young people he didn't recognize. He scanned them, trying to make sense of their faces. They reminded him how long it had been since he had spent time with his mother, father, and old friends, who all had scattered after graduation. The first few months of work had simultaneously lasted forever and finished in an instant.

"It's so crazy right now," Lizzy said. "The wedding is so soon, but we're pumped."

Ian nodded, half listening; he had become distracted. In the living room, within the crowd, one young man stood out, literally. He was towering, with thick muscles that hugged the cuffs of his shirt as he held a red plastic cup in one hand and a dangling pizza slice in the other. He had clear dark skin and a strong square jaw. Ian could not stop staring. Had he met him before? Maybe somewhere at school.

They were almost in the mix, almost with the man, when Ian was stopped by a light tap on his back.

"Ian? Is that *little* Ian?"

Lizzy and Ian turned. The woman's face provided only a weak link to memory, but he was certain of some things. She had aged, added a little weight, and wore more makeup than ever before. He also knew she was Lizzy's mother and that he had completely forgotten her name.

"That is me," he said. "Good to see you again."

She embraced him. "When I last saw you, you were *this tall*." She wildly waved her hand nearly all the way down to the floor and turned to Lizzy. "You told me he wasn't going to come!"

Lizzy shrugged. "Well, he's here! I'll be right back. I need some water."

Lizzy's mom smiled. "How's your mom? How are you?"

"She's great. I'm doing well. It's been great."

"That's great. I'm glad to hear that."

The two looked awkwardly at each other, as if both

expected the other to continue the conversation. Their pause revealed an unfortunate truth: They had nothing to discuss, nor did they care to. However, as the pressure of their silence peaked, Ian succumbed to its weight.

"So," he said, "what brought you to the city? The wedding is still a bit of a ways away, right?"

She half smiled. "I just wanted to see Lizzy. She's going through so much right now, and things can change so fast. I just wanted to make sure she was doing all right."

Lizzy returned with her cup in hand. "After this is over, I need to take a bubble bath or something. It's getting hot in here. Too many people."

"Are you sure you should?" Lizzy's mom asked. "I'm not so sure bubbles are good for you now."

"Mom, it's fine!" Lizzy snapped.

There was another moment of silence, until Lizzy's mom turned to Ian and asked, "Ian, have you met the lucky man yet?"

"Not yet. I'm looking forward to it."

"Let me grab him." She shouted, "Regi!"

From the crowd, the tall man turned to face them. As he strolled over, he stood with his back straight, his chest up, and his shoulders wide. He owned his every step, claiming the space in front of him, and after he cruised over, he stretched out his hand and said, "What's up, man."

What's... Up... Man

Each syllable hit like a brick. Ian stumbled back. His legs buckled, his mind strained.

The voice. His voice!

All at once, the sound of screeching metal and cries of a stranger flittered in his mind. He had heard this voice before. He was sure of it. It was powerful, smooth as water, strong as steel, unmistakable.

He had heard the voice in his dreams.

Ian stared at him, jarred, until he realized it had been a few seconds since Regi had spoken. "Nice… to meet you," he said in slow words, then reached out with a clammy right hand and met Regi's grasp.

The voice! Shadows raced across Ian's mind. He could hear the shouts, Regi's desperation so clearly. "*Wait!*" he had cried.

Regi squeezed Ian's hand and gave a wide smile. "Good to meet you too."

After the shake, Ian let his arm collapse to his side and kept his eyes locked on Regi.

Regi pulled his hand up and laughed. "Man, you got some sweaty palms."

Around him, Lizzy, her mom, and Regi chuckled, while Ian continued to stare. It was him, he was sure of it. The blurred man, the beggar, the voice. It was him. It was Regi.

The man. Lizzy. Adriana. The blonde. Javi.

Regi. Lizzy. Adriana. The blonde. Javi.

An anxious uncertainty spread down to Ian's stomach. Questions conquered every inch of what he could process. *How did I hear him? How did I see him? Where did he come from?* Ian knew he had never met him before in his life.

"So what do you think?"

Ian, reeled back into reality, faced Regi. "What?"

Regi grinned and laughed. "Man, you high or something? I asked, 'what do you think about the place?'" Regi stretched out his arms, presenting the apartment to Ian. The living room had a big wide-screen TV, clean beige walls, and a connected balcony that overlooked the sidewalk.

Ian glanced around. Lizzy and her mom were missing. In a low voice, he said, "It's nice. It's real nice."

"Yes, I think so. I'm quite fond of it. It's been a lot of work, but things are coming together."

"That sounds great…" Ian could feel beads of sweat emerging on his brow.

Maybe I saw him online. No, that wouldn't explain the voice.

Then he felt a hand touch his shoulder and instinctively flinched. Regi held on with a soft grip. "Hey man, you alright? You don't look so good."

Ian stepped back, letting Regi's hand slide off. For the first time, he stared directly at Regi, and Regi stared at him. He was large, with a wide face and a thick neck, but he wasn't intimidating. No, his gaze was friendly with warm brown eyes. He looked genuinely concerned.

"I'm… fine…" Ian checked to see if anyone was close enough to hear him. "I was just wondering… do you dream?"

Regi squinted and cocked his head. "Seriously, are you tripping?" He laughed. "Of course I dream. Why you ask?"

Ian sighed. "I just had this crazy dream… It's kind of hard to describe… It was really blurry, and there was this voice… and it sounded like your voice."

Regi crossed his arms, retaining his smile. "Huh. What did it say?"

Ian turned off to the side. "At first the voice was talking to its mother. It said, 'I just don't know, Mama.' Another time, it was begging this woman to not leave a church. It said, 'Don't go…'" Ian glanced back at Regi, whose brow was furrowed.

"What else happened?"

Ian's words quickened. "Well, in some grass, the voice said, 'Okay, Mama. I'm ready,' and the dream ended. In the church, the voice told a woman who was leaving, 'You forgot your keys,' and the dream ended. They were just such strange dreams, and to be honest, they reminded me of you."

Regi's firm gaze had lost focus. He rubbed his neck with the back of his hand, and right as he opened his mouth, Lizzy emerged from behind him.

"You look so serious. What are you guys talking about?"

Ian carefully examined her face.

Regi recovered smoothly. "Nothing, just dreams."

"Oh? What's your dream?" Lizzy asked.

"Hmm," Regi sighed and loosened the tight hold he had placed on himself. His shoulders dropped, and he wrapped his arm around Lizzy. "I'm not quite sure, but I'm getting pretty close, I think." Then he pulled her closer to him, nestling her body against his. Holding her under his arm, he turned his attention back to Ian and asked, "What about you, Ian, what's your dream?"

Ian gawked at him blankly. "I don't know."

Further drilling his gaze into Lizzy, Ian tried to connect memory with dream and dream with reality, and found only confusion. It went on like that for a bit, with Regi and Lizzy staring at him, while he stared at them, until Regi said, "Baby. Let's go catch up with my family." He waved at Ian, who still stared on. "It was nice to meet you."

"Nice to meet you as well," whispered Ian. The two walked away, and he was left staring at his feet.

The flare. The church. The rock. The roundabout. The collapse.

Regi. Lizzy. Adriana.

The blonde.

Javi.

He realized he needed to find her.

Ian pushed his way past Lizzy's friends and went back into the dining room where he found her. Lizzy's mom. He leapt forward and sat beside her. She smiled and said, "Hello!"

He puffed out, "Hi, I was wondering something, just a small question. Did Lizzy ever have short hair?"

She laughed. "Why do you ask?"

Ian blinked. "No reason. I thought I just saw a picture or something."

"Ah, I see," she said. "Yes, for a bit, when she moved to the city, she had this super-short hair. And honestly…" She leaned in and said quietly, "I didn't care for it too much." She started snickering, like she had revealed some inside joke. "I'm glad she got rid of it and let it grow back. It took a while, though."

Ian had grown pale. "What about Regi's mother? Who is she?"

"You're a very inquisitive one, aren't you?" Lizzy's mom frowned. "That's a sad story. She died last year. Brain aneurysm, I think. I never got to meet her."

Lizzy's mom continued, rattling off wedding plans, her tiny and not-so-tiny struggles, what she'd want out of potential grandchildren, but Ian clutched his sides and failed to fully absorb a single new word coming from her.

Regi… Ian had dreamed of Regi before he met him. *Why Regi?*

Strangers were being carried into his dreams.

Regi. Lizzy. Adriana. The blonde and Javi.

Ian's head burned. *Why is this happening?*

IAN WALKED out of Regi's apartment with a new intensity. He moved aimlessly down the street and crunched any dead leaf in sight. Even in the cold, he felt warm. A raw energy had been ignited.

He wandered, vaguely exploring the new neighborhood while taking in nothing. There was no hope in concentration; thoughts leapt in all directions from possibility to reality, all entirely unable to focus. His brain spun, his heart fluttered. The birth of newness had drifted into his life, driving an insatiable excitement. He smiled at cars vrooming around corners and at buildings that cast mighty shadows.

Then he stopped. The great confusion, the new adventure, reminded him of something he had stalled, but now the gates appeared open again. It was time for action.

He reached into his pocket, pulled out his phone, and with a blind certainty, found her contact and texted: *Hi.*

Moving again, he increased his pace, faster and faster, from a stroll to a walk to nearly a run. He would see this through, he decided. Something great was coming for him. At last, a buzz in his pocket interrupted the frenzy. He jumped at it. It read: *Hi.*

He stopped and stood straight. He didn't want to send the wrong message, but he also didn't want to put too much effort into the message, because then he'd overthink it, but he also couldn't underthink it and write something strange sounding, so maybe he would just opt to send a funny picture, but he decided against that because they didn't know each other like that, so he waffled back and forth, postulating, predicting, and proposing. Lunch, that was it! Lunch, he had said they would go to lunch. He typed: *Do you want to grab—*

A new message appeared. *Do you want to meet me in the park?*

Ian asked himself, *Do I want to go the park?* He looked to the sky and sniffed the air around him. He found gray clouds and frosty air. No, it was not the kind of day for park visiting, he thought, yet he found himself quickly sending: *When?*

Nowish? Like in 30? I was heading there.

Ian jogged toward the nearest subway station. *Ok I'll be there in 20.*

On the train, he found himself leaning against a pole while his chest pulsated. He flicked at his phone, delaying and hesitating before messaging: *Where in the park?*

He baked in a slow tension until she sent him a clue. *I'm biking up from 40th and 8th.*

Ian watched the silent strangers of the train and grinned to himself. It seemed he had escaped the stillness of his life, while they simply rode on.

Minutes later, he wrote: *I'm off the train.* He walked slowly toward the park, then he stopped and made his stand.

There, on a cobble corner where the street connected to the park, he waited. He looked out for her, expecting a massive shiny bike to emerge out of the busy streets, but he did not see one. After a minute, he worried that he wouldn't be able to recognize her. After three, he worried that she wouldn't come at all. To keep time moving, he people-watched. He had counted three couples pass by, strolling side by side in front of him, in and out of the park. Each looked like a perfect fit with the other, comfortable and cool in their partner's atmosphere. One even held hands.

Ian tugged at his shirt. Sweat had dampened his collar.

He gave up searching on the street and waddled toward the park. Perhaps she had already arrived. His nervous migration led him to an ice cream stand where an ice cream man stood still, with a scarf wrapped around his neck and a hat over his head, revealing only his eyes, nose, and lips. Every few seconds, he would break the frozen hold on himself and turn to peer at the passing pedestrians before returning to his stationary pose. *Did he have a vague hope that someone would want ice cream in winter, or did he just have nothing better to do?*

At least the park's outermost trees stood tall behind Ice Cream Man, providing him company during the frigid day. They were held back by small metal gates while they flexed their naked limbs, free from the weight of summer leaves. As they swayed, they warned all newcomers: *stay wary.*

Ian traced them from root to trunk to crown to sky, a sky which was already graying. The day had barely dipped into afternoon, but already it felt like evening. Every day was growing darker quicker.

"Hi, is that you, Ian?"

His brain spat and stuttered. He snapped himself around, and there she was.

Hallie.

"Hi. It's good to see you." He smiled, but she did not. She wheeled a light-blue bike on the ground, and her forehead was coated with glistening sweat, which only made her look more alive.

She nudged her head. "Come on, let's go."

She started walking toward the park and managed to get a few feet away before Ian fully digested the moment. He sprinted to catch up.

They walked in silence together as they slipped deeper into the City's miniature forest. Looking at it in his nervous state of heightened awareness, he realized that he had never really looked at it, only passed by. Careful architects had managed to weave meadow with metropolitan and cement with country. To his right, a massive boulder rested, glued in the ground, and a young boy reigned on top of it while his father watched him from behind. To Hallie's left, an open field showed off new brown patches, grass dead from winter. And straight ahead, bikers zipped past an artificial lake and squirrels dashed behind the metal fences, scurrying from tree to tree.

Ian wanted to say something to her, to tell her how glad he was to see her again, to tell her that something fantastic was happening to him, but before he could, she spoke for him.

"So, what do you do?"

He thought momentarily. "I'm a consultant."

"What does that mean?"

"I tell other companies what to do, specifically for their websites."

"So what do you do?"

Ian offered a puzzled face. "I just told you. I tell others what to do."

"It sounds like you don't do much of anything."

He awkwardly shrugged. "It isn't too bad."

"Well, is your advice good? Do they listen?"

"Sometimes, I guess." He put his left hand on the top of his head and rustled his hair.

"What advice have you been giving?"

"Honestly," said Ian, "I think you'd find it boring."

Hallie glared at him. "Maybe. You don't know that."

He frowned. She was right. He didn't know that. "I guess you're right. We're helping a paper company redesign their website."

The two turned a corner and found two benches carved into the heart of the park, next to the bike path.

"No, you were right, that does sound boring. Let's go over there."

He followed her. "Well, what do *you* do?"

"I do a lot of things. I read, I draw." Hallie lifted her bike. "I bike."

"What do you do for work, though?"

"I haven't been doing much work recently. I've been taking classes and making things on the side."

The two sat down on the bench, and Ian watched Hallie as she spoke. She stared ahead, seeming to enjoy the bikers and joggers and wind chill. "I've been getting into sculpting lately."

"Do you want to be doing that forever, though?"

With a sudden intensity, she asked, "Why are you talking about forever? It's what I'm doing right now."

He searched for an answer to her question but couldn't find one.

Together, they sat and watched the day drain away and the City flow by. He tried to find comfort on the bench, but the cold metal railings pressed into his side, and the shifting wind brushed against his ears. He fidgeted around, staring at the City's winter and the dull of the day, searching for things to say.

Then Hallie whispered, "Look at that."

She spoke nearly muted, like each word could shatter the peace. She pointed at a bush. In front of them, hiding behind a tiny awning of trees, a small cat tiptoed across the soil. "Isn't that nice?" she asked.

Looking at the cat, its scruffy, ugly fur, all he could think was how miserable it must be, how cold, how tired. It might not even survive the winter. "I guess so," said Ian. "I would've never noticed him."

"I think it's a her," she said.

He turned to Hallie. It seemed like the cold didn't bother her at all. Sure, she had a hat and gloves, but so did he, and he was frozen. She didn't flinch, nor did she shiver. It was as if she could make anywhere her home, any season. Winter was just another novelty; she studied the world with a constant curiosity as its companion, and in turn the world looked back at her the same.

He exhaled and asked, "Hallie, what do you think of dreams?"

Finally, Hallie turned to face him. She stared right into his eyes with no hesitation. By reflex, he avoided her gaze and instead focused on a cloud drifting slightly above.

"What do you mean?"

He felt a lump in his throat. "Dreams. What do you think about them?"

"You ask some strange questions," she said. Then she spent a while to ponder it. "I don't know. But I guess it depends on the dream, and the dreamer. Also depends on what you want out of the dream."

"But do you think they mean something?"

"Maybe. Maybe not. I usually forget mine."

"Oh."

Silence regained its foothold between them, while the ambient noise of cars, bikers, pedestrians, and wind spread over their lull. Time gently wore on, and when Ian looked to the sun once more, it was almost completely consumed by night.

Hallie tapped the bench. "I think I'm going to go back to biking. I'll see you later."

"What?" He leaned in closer. "We just got here. Why did you say we should meet up if you're just going to leave?"

She shrugged. "It was convenient. I was already out biking."

He slightly shook his head as he searched for words. "Why were you biking?"

She stood above him and said, "I guess I was bored."

Ian watched as she started running, gained momentum, and then hopped onto the blue bike.

"Let's get drinks sometime," she shouted, then started pedaling.

After he gave a weak wave goodbye, she was gone.

Somewhere out of sight, Adriana softly asked, "*¿Dónde estoy?*"

Ian squinted. The sun was bright and shot its rays directly onto the back of his neck. In the air, a mild warmth coupled with a cool breeze to make an invisible ally, which soothed his skin. He blinked and looked around, lost.

He was standing on a hill, next to scattered patches of desert grass atop arid, cracked earth. At the bottom of the hill, he spotted a small river slowly marching forward to a faraway freedom.

Then he heard Adriana ask once more, "Where am I?"

He moved away from the river and toward her voice. He spotted her sitting on a chair on a lawn outside a tiny beige adobe home, while she stared down at the river's basin.

Ian moved closer and gazed at the home. The dry air had caked into its walls; it told its history by means of aged cracks and abrasions. And standing in the home's open door, a hunched man faced away from them. He said, "*Sabes,*" then repeated, "You know."

Ian peered at Adriana. Something about her had changed.

She was still old, but she was slightly younger. Some wrinkles had dissipated, some hair had come back. She no longer seemed so completely lost and confused, only a little out of place. She sat, holding the sides of her wooden chair, while staring ahead with an empty gaze.

Walking toward her, Ian purposefully stepped in front of her view, but she did not react. She simply stared.

"I don't know. I don't remember," she said.

The man raised his voice and said, "You're here. You're home."

Ian found the hunched figure curious, hiding himself from them. He appeared shrunken and held his body tight together as he wrapped his arms around his torso. His exposed neck was impossibly shriveled, more sandpaper than skin, and with a raspy and shrill voice, he spoke like he barely wanted to say anything.

"Oh," Adriana said.

For a bit, the two remained silent, and instead let the river's flow trickle into their ears. Then in a confused voice, Adriana asked, "You aren't here anymore, isn't that right?"

"I'm here!" the man snapped. "I'm right here!"

"Oh," she repeated.

Ian looked beyond the home. Many more tiny adobe houses dotted the landscape, all positioned beside a gray road, which carried on into the distance.

The ancient man, still facing away, mumbled, "It's you who's not here anymore. You're somewhere else, somewhere north."

"Oh, where's that?"

The man did not answer. Instead, he asked, "Where's my baby? I need to speak to him."

Adriana touched the side of her head. "Who?"

The man spat onto the dusty ground. He fidgeted and held

the side of the home to support himself. "Brother! Brother! Brother!" he exclaimed.

Adriana held her head. "I don't know. I can't remember."

Ian approached Adriana. She had broken her gaze and seemed to be searching for something that he couldn't see. *What?* Ian wondered. *What is she trying to remember?*

She began scratching at her sides, then stood up and paced around.

Ian shivered. The wind had picked up and blew past him and rippled Adriana's dress. He rechecked the landscape. The sky had become overcast.

The old man pushed himself off the adobe wall and reached his arms up. They were dark brown, baked permanently by the sun, and although his body was tiny, he cast a long shadow, which stretched out past Adriana and reached all the way to Ian's feet. "Where is he?" he shouted.

"I don't know, I don't know," Adriana said as she paced.

In the earth, the air, the dream, Ian could sense her energy rising. Her intensity came as a faint rumble, a new wind, an intimidating quiet, as her chaotic cognition spilled out into tangibility. He tightened his legs and set his feet into the dirt. He would be ready this time.

She walked back and forth and back again, until she stopped. She raised her head and looked to the river. Ian turned as well and saw that something indeed had changed.

The river had picked up its pace. Down in the basin, it screamed as large bubbles gurgled and exploded on its surface. Ian held himself steady, reasoning it was just Adriana's overactive imagination, that it was only a dream.

Then an arm reached out of its waters.

In one stroke, the blonde woman pulled herself out of the river with her hair intact and her makeup pristine. She stared at Adriana as she began her march up the hill.

Adriana stopped pacing and instead began to rattle. She

pointed down at the woman and screamed, "Go away! Go away! Go away! I hate you!"

The blonde woman did not respond; she only continued to march. Under Ian, the earth began to shiver and tremble. He felt an urge to run, but there was nowhere to go, nor would his fear allow him to move. Adriana's panic had spiked and her terror appeared to be overflowing, reaching his heart as well.

The old man's shadow had grown into an overcast storm, which completely shrouded the pair of Ian and Adriana in darkness. "Where is my baby?" he demanded.

She turned to him and screamed, "Papá, I'm here! I'm here!"

"Not you!" Papá screamed. Then he turned around.

Ian's heart stopped, panic rattled his spine, dread flooded his mind. *Some things are just not meant to be seen*, he realized instantly.

The man's face was contorted and twisted. It resembled a broken mess, like someone had melted down his features and forgotten what he had originally looked like when they attempted to put him back together. His nose curved down, his eyes were too close together, and his mouth slanted sideways. Everything about him seemed sloppy, squished, pained, unsightly, and disturbed.

Adriana looked toward the ground as her focus fragmented between Papá and the blonde woman, who now ran toward them. "I don't know!" she shouted. "I don't know!"

Papá began to walk to them, and as he moved, his shadow curled and twirled, pushing and pulling itself on the earth. Ian took a few steps back and looked toward the river, but there the blonde woman continued her approach with blaring red eyes, sunken cheeks, and concentrated hate. He had nowhere to go.

Ancient and angry, Papá walked up to Adriana and grabbed her. By the time he reached her, his face had become one with his shadows, wrapping themselves around him, covering his features in darkness. His nose, eyes, and mouth all oozed together, like a growing puddle of dark water, blackened by dirt and grime, until he was unrecognizable. What he once was had been lost and forgotten, replaced by a contaminated shadow of a memory, leaving only a blob of nothingness in its place.

The ground began to violently shift, and Ian fell, while the sound of the train emerged loud and clear. The old man's words rolled together with the metal screeching and became distorted, almost incomprehensible. "You should've stopped her," he said.

Ian looked back to the blonde woman—she was closing in, now only yards away.

Adriana closed her eyes and shook her head. "This isn't right, this isn't right."

He watched the old man grow taller and taller, until he towered over them. Ian followed Adriana's lead and clutched his ears and closed his eyes. The sounds, the sights had become piercing, painful. He waited for the dream to collapse into darkness as it did before, suddenly and violently.

Then he heard a final, metallic shout from the old man that cut through the air, cut through the earth, and cut through his skin. "*Javi!*" the man screamed.

And all at once, that unstoppable rumble slowed down to a stop, and the shrill metal roar ceased. Cautiously, Ian opened his eyes. Papá, the man with the forgotten face, had melted into the shadows, with the last traces of him oozing into the ground. The blonde woman was also missing, while the landscape faded.

Adriana fell backward. She had slipped; her weight had taken over her body. She tipped over and said, "You're gone, and I'm not there."

Ian tried to move to her to catch her, but she was too far away, and he was nudged back by something.

He turned around and saw walls had materialized around them and the arid grass beneath their feet had turned into wooden planks. Above them, the sky turned from blue to black, and then into a gray ceiling.

The landscape had transformed and dragged them along its reinvention, from sights unseen to sights seen. Within just moments, Ian and Adriana were back in an apartment room, a bedroom with white walls. She fell back onto the bed and whispered, "I'm here."

Ian breathed and held his hand over his heart. He had been hyperventilating, he realized, but now his heart rate was returning to normal. In the interim, the sound of the train resumed, shaking the earth once more.

Adriana held her head close and kept her eyes closed, and Ian watched all things begin to disappear except Adriana, the bed, him, and the sound of the train. First, the floor under them vanished, and they succumbed to the slow gravity of the abyss.

While he fell, he inspected Adriana on her bed and studied the dissipating space. His fear had left him, replaced by an intense curiosity. He realized he had been in that room before.

Finally, she mumbled, "Nothing's here," and even she faded, as well as her bed. Soon all that was left was the sound of the train, until it trailed off, leaving behind silence.

By the end of it, all that surrounded Ian was darkness. Simple and straightforward darkness.

CHAPTER SEVEN

"What can I do for you today?" Oscar asked as he sat across his desk with a smile glued to his face and his hands nestled in his lap.

"I wanted to talk about the project," said Ian. He twiddled his thumbs and stared at the back of his hands, finding himself lost in their every pore and crevice while he traced the veins that pumped blood into his arms and observed how pale he had become since his arrival in the City.

"What about it?"

Oscar kept smiling. Ian had taught himself to distrust that smile, always appearing too pleasant. More likely it was an annoyed intensity boiling beneath the surface.

"To be honest, I wanted to talk about my role," said Ian, sighing. "I don't think the team needs me." He paused, letting the words float throughout the room and weigh down the space. "The communication isn't great, and Rohan and Zoey are doing a great job. They don't need me."

As he watched the world turn behind a glass window, Ian barely avoided Oscar's gaze.

"Is that so?"

He offered a weak nod. "I'd like to do something else, go somewhere I'm more needed, somewhere I can create more impact. I can do more," said Ian. He leaned back in the chair and relaxed some, feeling like a weight had been lifted.

Oscar looked up to the ceiling and said nothing. He shifted his torso in his custom ergonomic swivel chair and tapped his right black shoe against the ground. Then he focused straight in at Ian, chuckled, and spoke all at once.

"Ian, Ian, Ian! Here's the problem: You need to push. You need to show how needed you are. Show how much value you can add. Get up and grind," Oscar said while he vigorously shook his head. "That's the way to do it." He stood up and raised his hand into the air. "That said, I know how you feel. I've felt the same."

Ian looked up at Oscar. He had begun to pace.

"Maybe it'd help to realize you're at a beginning of a great journey," he said, "but that's the key word—*beginning*." Then Oscar stopped, grabbed his desk, and stared directly at Ian.

"This is a great client to start with. Very nice people. Also Zoey, Rohan, they're the dream team. They're brilliant. They're a great team. You're young and haven't worked for long. Don't worry too much about running ahead of yourself. Realize you're building something. You need some skills first; you're just beginning."

Ian began to slide down in his chair, letting his legs dip to the floor while his bottom hung halfway off. Oscar grabbed the side of his chair, threw himself back on it, rolled forward, and leaned on his desk.

"Let me tell you a story, okay?"

Ian said nothing.

"Okay," Oscar said, "I'll tell you the story. My father told me this story when I first started working, when I was picking up dogshit from hot pavement all summer for all the people too lazy to walk their own damn dogs. It has guided me ever since."

Ian began to track a bird that landed on the windowsill of a building across the block. It was brown and tiny, barely big enough to count as a bird at all.

"It goes like this," Oscar said. "There was a man. A young man, extremely smart, very capable. He left home to go somewhere far away, on a great journey, and was thrilled. It was going to be great, he was going to be great, he thought! But there was a problem. He walked along the road and eventually met a giant mountain, which blocked his path. It was enormous! You listening?"

Ian nodded at the bird. He had seen a bird in that one dream with the roundabout.

"Okay, so, the man was deciding what to do and realized he had two options."

Oscar raised his pointer finger. "One: he could try to climb over the mountain and get to the other side."

Oscar raised his middle finger. "Or two: He could go sideways. What do you think he ended up doing?"

"I'm not sure," Ian mumbled.

"Well, think about it. You're being paid to think."

The bird flew away and disappeared out of sight. "He went sideways?"

"That's right. He went sideways! He tried to go *around* the mountain. But soon he met another mountain along the path, and again, instead of climbing it, instead of facing the challenge, he went sideways. Again, and again, sideways, sideways. Always searching for an easier way, never walking forward, never walking straight. In the end, all he ever did was go sideways and walk in a great big circle, back where he started. Just older, a lot older."

Oscar paused. "You see what I mean, Ian?" He began to speak softly, almost more to himself than anybody else. "You don't want to be the guy who goes sideways, who gets distracted and gives up."

He turned to face his employee. "So don't fret. Just keep on hammering."

Ian nodded like he understood Oscar's words, but somewhere in the midst of the story he had lost his concentration. Since the bird had flown away, he had resorted to watching Oscar's shadows dance as he spoke. They brought him back to his most recent dream.

"That makes a lot of sense. Thanks for the story," Ian said, then he stretched his legs, straightened his back, and stood up.

Oscar rocked into the back of his chair. "No problem, and don't worry. Thanks for talking to me. Everything will be great." Ian began to leave when Oscar asked, "Can you close the door behind you, please?"

After he walked out, Ian gently pulled the door shut, letting it click to a close, and began to walk away. But then he stopped. He turned to face its white paint and stared at it. Behind it, he could swear he heard the whisper of a great groan.

IAN ARRIVED HOME LATE. He fell onto his bed, leaned on his side, then stretched his neck toward his window. The glass had fogged up and was rattling against the wind. Already it was dark. He realized he hadn't felt the sun that entire day.

He collapsed and closed his eyes. Walking over the dreams once again, he tried to piece together what he had seen.

Regi begging, Lizzy drowning, Adriana screaming.

Each dream held secrets, elusive truths far more fascinating than anything he experienced while awake. Already he had seen into Regi's, Lizzy's, and Adriana's minds, and in spite of the impossible images, every second felt authentic, clear as a dive into their souls, all full of anxiety, doubt, and fear.

He had determined that their dreams had progressed into

each other. First he had experienced Regi's, which flowed into Lizzy's, which led into Adriana's, but *how* and *why* still evaded him.

How was this happening?

Why him? Why was he their receiver?

And where was Javi?

It kept going: *How, why, what, where, when, how, why, what, where, when, how, why, what, where, when, how...*

It seemed to never end. *Why, what, where, when, how, why, what, where, when, how, why, what, where, when, how, why, what, where, when, how, why, what, where, when, how, why, what, where, when, how, why, what, where, when, how, why, what, where, when, how, why, what, where, when, how, why, what, where, when, how...*

Perhaps it never would. *Why, what, where, when, how, why, what, where, when, how, why, what, where, when, how, why, what, where, when, how, why, what, where, when, how, why, what, where, when, how, why, what, where, when, how, why, what, where, when, how, why, what, where, when, how, why, what, where, when, how, why, what, where, when, how, why, wha—*

But then the torrent abruptly stopped. The room's silence broke his concentration. He hadn't realized that he had fallen into an utter stillness, with no sounds of construction or engine revs blasting through his window. For a moment, he was alone, in a quiet with himself.

It didn't sit right.

He glanced around, looking for something to hold, and a metallic shine caught his eye. He lurched over his bed and grabbed his phone. Then he began to scroll and found two messages:

The first was an email from Zoey: *Good job, team. I heard back from the client. The presentation is on for Monday. Meeting time is*

6:45 a.m., outside the office. We're getting a rental to drive up. Best, Zoey.

The news filled Ian with a passive, mild joy. At least he was inching closer to something new, a new project, a new website. But then another thought stirred. He checked the date and realized it had already been two months since he moved to the City.

Unbelievable. Then he continued to scroll.

The second message was a text from Lizzy. He had seen it pop up earlier but had ignored it to instead study something a little lighter, an article labeled: "5 Reasons You Feel So Tired."

She had written: *I don't want to be weird, but did you say something to Regi? You were really weird around him... After the party he told me you were an "interesting" guy, and then he started acting really strange...*

I guess I just want to know if there's a problem. I don't want negative energy from my own family only a few weeks from my wedding.

As he read it, he wanted to shrink under his covers. Then he did so. He wrapped his blanket tight over his head and hid underneath; he could have hidden there for a lifetime.

The message tugged at his stomach. He regretted saying anything at the party. Trying to hide in his phone, he desperately scrolled past timelines and feeds, without even reading what had passed.

On and on he went, scrolling, looping and looping, until, without even noticing, he slowly unwound. He slowed, slowed... and slowed, until he found himself at an absolute standstill.

Yes, he remembered, *Regi's dreams flowed into Lizzy's, which flowed into Adriana's.*

He sat back up and bent over his phone. This wasn't a mistake. No, this was an *opportunity*. He needed to see Lizzy. Now he had the perfect opening.

Planning and plotting, he wrote:

My bad! I liked talking to Regi, didn't mean to rub him the wrong way. I'm really happy for you guys.

He stopped, fiddled with his phone, and continued: *Also, can we talk?*

Then he deleted everything and began again:

My bad! Regi's great. It was good seeing you all. By the way, is there a time where we could get lunch? I'd love to talk to you and Regi more. I'm still trying to meet people out here, and it was a ton of fun hanging out with you guys!

He read the message twice, tapped send, and went to the bathroom. There he faced the mirror with an unfocused gaze and looked past his reflection. The recent words of Hallie and Oscar, their shaky wisdoms, lingered in his ears. However, they did not last. His scattered concentration quickly pulled him toward another direction.

Regi. Lizzy. Adriana. The blonde. Javi. And even *Papá.*

Their faces flickered in his mind; their voices murmured in his gray matter. His attention twitched from dream to dream, clouding everything else. Every night presented more questions and fewer answers.

Staring into the bathroom's darkness, lost in unstable thinking, Ian readied himself. He needed to know what was happening.

It was time to find some answers.

The first thing Ian noticed was the moon's glow and the dozen or so stars that floated around it. They shined brilliantly through the night sky, raining comfort onto the terrain. As he stretched his muscles, he breathed, inhaling dry air and warm wind and exhaling quiet. Around him were humble homes, simple grassy plains, and the melody of the river's current. He was back.

From atop Adriana's hill, he watched the moon's reflection on the river, how its image moved and morphed with the water's flow. Bending over, he touched the caked earth. This time, he could feel its dust. Now every touch felt authentic; it all had become so real.

"*Bajemos.*"

Ian turned to the sound coming from upstream—a bundle of laughter. He walked down the hill to the river and turned a corner. Ahead of him he saw two grinning girls, young teenagers who stood beside a docked rowboat.

One of them climbed over the side of the boat and gently took the hand of the other. She asked, "You ready?"

"I don't know," the other sheepishly said but climbed in anyway, then the two worked to unhook the rope that kept the boat tethered to land.

Ian sped up, trying to get closer to them. He huffed down the riverbank stopping suddenly when he saw her for who she was.

The uncertain girl in the boat, somehow, some way, was the frenetic Adriana he had come to know. She had the same eyes, generally the same shape, yet the two were also impossibly different. This girl couldn't have been more than fourteen. She still had smooth skin, which glowed under the moon's shine, and a face free from time's punishment. She was still young, still overflowing with life.

Adriana grinned and laughed. "You're crazy."

The other girl shrugged. "Night is a perfect time for a boat ride."

As the current carried them forward, Ian followed them. They sat in silence for a minute, and only the sound of the river and crickets filled the valley, but Ian could sense more. He felt everything: the air's purity, the riverbank's smooth stones under his feet, and his body's weight. Mesmerized by the serenity, he relaxed. There was nothing he needed to do, nowhere he needed to be. He had his peace.

Eventually, the silence was broken. "María," Adriana asked, "did you hear what happened?" Her voice was soft and uncertain.

María smiled at her. "It's okay."

She took Adriana's left hand and leaned in closer and whispered into her ear. Ian approached the river's edge, but even there they were too far away; he couldn't hear them.

Adriana smiled and giggled.

Then María grinned and stood. "Look, look over there!" She pointed toward the top of the hill, and out of the night's shadow, a small figure appeared, a young boy. He ran toward them and smiled and waved. "Adi! Adi!" he shouted. "I found her."

Adi, Adriana, stood up and asked, "Javi, where did you come from?"

Javi!

Ian began to desperately study him. He was just a *boy*, a boy with long wild hair and bright-green eyes and an unstoppable energy. As Javi ran down the hill toward the side of the river, he laughed and jumped and shouted. His joy made Ian smile; his glee appeared contagious. He waved to the girls while they smiled at him.

María turned to Adi. "See? I told you. He's right here! He's here."

"I guess you're right," she whispered.

Ian approached Javi, drawn in by his vitality, but then he stopped. He spotted a second figure following the boy down the hill.

A shiver slipped through his spine, and an ache touched his brain. He could tell by his size, by his gait—on the hill was Papá.

Ian clenched his fists as Papá approached, and Ian ambled toward him, preparing for another storm, but as he grew closer, Ian saw he wasn't frightening at all. In this dream, Papá was far younger than the previous, maybe forty at most, and no monster, no mangled face or oozing shadows, only a man. A tanned man with tired eyes.

He looked at the two girls with a solemn frown. "María, go to your house. No more of this."

María let go of Adi's hands and turned to her. "Adi, let's do this again."

Adi nodded and smiled.

Grinning, Javi looked back at the hill and laughed. "Relax, Papá," he said. "It's all good."

Adi stretched herself out and rested her head against the

prow of the boat. Then she began to laugh. She laughed to the point where her body shook and heaved against the ship. Her excitement would not allow itself to be contained. As Ian watched her, he unconsciously cracked another smile. Around her, María grew still and began to fade. Javi quickly dissipated too, along with Papá.

He expected an end at any moment, for the train to carry them away, but it did not come. He waited long seconds, and Adi, the boat, and the river remained. The night became filled with her echoing laughter, and he noticed the water under the boat was shifting. It had been smooth waves before, but now it was bumping, pushing, condensing. It assumed long regular rectangular shapes, all connected to one another. Then it hardened, browned, and solidified. In just moments, the river went from a smooth stream to a wooden floor with the boat sitting on top of it.

Ian walked onto the planks and leaned down to touch them, but then he felt something hard brush against his back. He turned and saw a white wall had begun to climb out of the wooden river's edge. It was born slowly but grew quickly, reaching its final height in a matter of moments, and then began to push forward toward the edge of floor, carrying Ian along with it. While it carried him forward, he could see three similar walls had sprouted on the wooden river. Together, the four walls formed a rectangle, encasing him, Adi, and the boat together. Then a slab extended out of their sides, forming a roof, and a door appeared on one of the walls.

In a short time, the scene was complete, and it was familiar. Ian grinned. He even clapped. At long last, he knew where they were, where they had returned for all of Adriana's dreams. They were back in Lizzy's old bedroom, back in the City.

Soon young Adi's laughter slowed down, and the boat's

shape changed. A mattress filled its hull, which pushed Adi up, and its prow turned into a headrail. Adi smiled and swung her legs off the edge of the bed, letting them dangle.

Waiting together, they both watched the room's doorknob slowly turn. Then the door opened, and there was Adriana, the older Adriana Ian knew.

She looked better than when he had first met her groaning on the side of the road, more put together, less shaky. She walked in and sat next to young Adi. Then she turned to her. "I forgot what María said. Can you tell me?"

Adi giggled. "You should know!" The girl began to laugh again, with her stomach busting up and down. "If I can remember, you can too!"

"How can you laugh at a time like this, with what just happened?" Adriana demanded. She sighed. "You don't know anything."

Adi rose from the bed and strolled toward the door before stopping mid-pace. She turned back to face Adriana. "Clearly I remember more than you," she said, then she laughed louder than ever, and the sound of a train began to roll in, emerging between her chuckles.

Adriana gave up a small smile. "I still remember that night."

As Adi laughed, her hands melted into the air, and her body vanished. Soon the ascension of the train replaced her laugh and filled the room. The walls and the floor turned into nothingness, leaving behind only Ian, the bed, and old Adriana. They began to fall, gently drifting into space. Adriana gazed at where the door had once been and then dissipated into oblivion, along with the bed frame, until finally the mattress disappeared.

Ian watched it all in a quiet peace, holding a great calm in his chest. He knew what he needed to ask Lizzy.

He heard the train echoing everywhere throughout the folds of the void. He smiled. The rattle filled the emptiness, surrounding him, embracing him. Dream was all there ever was, he told himself, and all he would ever need.

CHAPTER EIGHT

"What did you want to talk about?"

It had taken Lizzy three days to respond to Ian's request. She had agreed to meet him for lunch on Sunday at a Thai restaurant near her apartment but told him it would be impossible for Regi to come. He was far too busy with work.

Dressed in a baggy sweater, she had ordered a double extra-large helping of pineapple fried rice. "Hold the sauce," she had said. Now, even though she sat directly across from Ian, she looked at him only out of the corner of her eye while shifting in her chair.

He forced a smile. "It's good to see you too." Then he said in a hushed tone, "Honestly, I was just wondering about something. It's not a big deal."

"What?" she demanded.

Ian wanted to describe the dreams. He wanted to unleash the sights, sounds, and weave them all into a great tapestry and take her on his journey, but he didn't know where to start, where to begin to describe what was happening. Instead, as he faced Lizzy during the day, his mind only stuttered and spluttered and stopped.

Lizzy caught his blank stare and grabbed onto the moment of weakness.

"Let me tell you something," she said. "You hesitated to shake Regi's hand. I think I even saw you start to sweat. I'll ask you again: Do you have a problem with Regi? Are you racist or something? Maybe just a psycho?" Her voice made it clear that she wasn't posing a question. She was staging an interrogation.

"W-what?" he stammered.

"I'm marrying that man," she said as she held herself close. "I love him. If you have a problem with him, don't talk to me."

A sudden cold confusion in Ian's gut rapidly burned into anger. "I don't have a problem with Regi. Is that what he told you?"

Lizzy shook her head. "He didn't need to tell me anything. He just said you were funny, and he started acting strange after the party. I asked him what was up, and he told me he didn't want to talk about it. Then he disappeared for a day and said, 'I wanted to talk to my dad.' It was weird. Regi gets along with everybody, and I could tell by the way you looked at him there was a problem. *You* were the problem. So tell me—what's the problem?"

Ian raised his voice. "I have no problem with Regi. There was just a question I needed to ask him."

"What?" Lizzy shouted.

"You order pineapple fried rice and flounder with side of soup?" The two turned. A woman smiled at them with two plates in hand.

"Yeah, they're ours," Lizzy murmured.

The woman put the plates down and grinned at them. "You know how long I work this week?"

"How long?" Lizzy grumbled.

The woman laughed. "Seventy-five-hour week."

Ian crossed his arms, and Lizzy said, "That sucks."

The woman shrugged and smiled. "Lesson: Sometimes it best to not worry." And she walked away.

The two ate in silence. While he chewed, Ian poked at the flounder filet in front of him and contemplated everything it had taken for it to get there onto his plate. It had come so far: explored seas and dodged predators, rode underneath the waves and swam with siblings, explored the bottom of the ocean and hunted to survive. All until it faced one bad day. Meanwhile, all he had done was poke at a website and try not to fall asleep.

"Let me ask you something, Lizzy. Have you ever had crazy dreams?"

She put her fork down. "What?"

His pace quickened. "Like really vivid dreams, like you were watching a movie?"

"What are you talking about?"

His hands shook, and his heart raced.

"Listen, Lizzy, just listen for once. I had this dream and saw you. You were in an ocean. You were carrying this rock. And it grew, it kept growing, and it dragged you down! I had a dream where you were drowning, Lizzy. I screamed at you to let go of the rock, but you didn't do it, and I still don't understand why."

Lizzy glared at him, mystified. She put the fork down and looked up at the ceiling, her focus scattered. Ian saw it. He had pierced her.

She lowered her voice and said, "That's weird. What else did you dream?"

"So do you remember that dream? The rock?"

Lizzy said nothing, and he waited, then spoke slower. "There was another dream where you were driving. I recognized your car... and buildings growing from the grass."

Lizzy looked down at the table and retightened her posture.

"And there was a woman in the road. She was old and had

a Spanish accent. She kept mumbling, 'Javi, Javi.' Do you remember that, Lizzy?"

Lizzy only dipped her head. He had trapped her in some kind of spell, or a curse. For once she did not know what to say, and even if she did, she wouldn't know how to say it. So instead, she trembled and asked, "What have you been… spying on me?"

"No."

She rubbed her eyes with the back of her hand, pushing back tears. "I barely know you. I don't know what your problem is, but honestly, dude, I think you should worry about your own life. Leave mine alone."

Her words hit like deadweight. They sucked the air out of Ian's lungs, silencing him. He scanned her face and his food while she slowly regained her composure.

He switched to his soup, and his dirty reflection stared back at him. He begrudgingly sipped the liquid. It wasn't what he had ordered.

"I have enough going on," Lizzy said. "I'm getting married in two weeks, my mom is constantly harassing me…" She paused and looked down. "And none of Regi's family even likes me."

"That's a shame," said Ian.

"Hell yeah, it's a *shame*." She shook her head and rubbed her temples. "I don't know what Regi told you, but I faintly remember some dream with a stone. Some nightmare."

Without hesitation, Ian's heart began to beat once again. "When did you have it?"

Lizzy wrapped her arms around her stomach, embracing herself. "A few months ago."

Ian's eyes widened. "A few months ago?"

"Yes, a few months ago." She blinked back her tears and sat up straight. "Yes, actually, that was when I told Regi it was now or never."

"Now or never?"

"To lock it up. We've been together for like, two years. He can be a little unsure. Sometimes you just got to push him."

Ian glanced at Lizzy's left hand. On her finger rested a brilliant diamond, which managed to reflect even the restaurant's dim fluorescent yellow.

Inspecting the gem with curiosity, he asked, "So you had that dream with the stone?"

"Yes, that's what I told you!" Lizzy snapped.

Ian couldn't help but smile at her. "Aren't you the least bit interested in how I know about it?"

It seemed like she was going to say something, by the way she moved, but then she shook her head. "Honestly, no. I couldn't care less. I have too many things to focus on. Clearly you don't."

"Okay, fine. Just tell me you're sure you don't know any Spanish lady," he said. "She'd be older, a lot older."

"I know my friend Anna speaks Spanish, but she's twenty-four."

"That's not her."

Lizzy glared at Ian. "Obviously." She closed her eyes. "There was this woman I met a long time ago. A couple years ago."

"Who?"

Lizzy opened her eyes and barked, "Can you just wait and let me speak? Damn."

After a pause, she said, "Thank you. There was this old Mexican lady. At least I think she was Mexican. I only saw her for a few hours. I was taking over her apartment. She was supposed to be gone by the time I showed up, but she was still there with all her stuff."

Adriana.

"Leave? Where was she going?"

Lizzy shook her head. "I don't know."

"What did she look like?"

"I don't remember. Her English wasn't the best. She was old, and maybe a little cuckoo. She ended up leaving all her furniture behind, which was fine by me. I just took it all. When I met her, I tried to tell her to leave, but she only mumbled to herself and kept wandering around. Finally, her friend came and removed her."

"You took all her furniture? Her bed, her mattress, everything?"

"Yes, are you deaf? That's what I just said."

"Was her name Adriana?"

"I don't know. It could've been."

Ian's mind was going a mile a minute.

"What about a dream with a church? Or a dream with a blonde woman? Do you remember any of those? Who was her friend?"

Lizzy held up her palm facing Ian, silently yelling, *Stop.*

He tried to calm down while she nibbled her rice, but his body naturally leaned forward. After her second bite, she gently put her fork down and faced him.

"Nope," she said. "I have no idea what you're talking about." She chuckled to herself and tossed another chunk of pineapple into her mouth, gnashing while she said, "I guess I see why Regi said you were a little funny after all. What's wrong with you? Why do you care so much about all of this?"

His mind began to gyrate. She met her a few years ago.

"Honestly…" He trailed off. "I'm just looking for something more interesting to do than wait for the subway."

Ian realized he had been looking at it all wrong. They hadn't been dreams of the future, nor the present. No, his journey had been backward. Each night he had been digging, digging into buried wonders, digging into forgotten treasures, digging farther and farther back into time, digging into old dreams.

A wide smile crept across his face. He couldn't help it. Everything was becoming clear.

STUMBLING ON HIS FEET, Ian arrived at home out of breath. He threw his door open, crashing it against the wall, and pounced forward onto his bed. He ripped its sheet off its corners, tearing it from its peace. It stunk of sweat and grime; he hadn't washed it since he moved in. He scrunched it into a ball and threw it onto the floor. Then, breathing heavily, he stood and admired his work.

It was a mattress, still ugly, still gray, still stained with unsightly yellow and reddish hues, still with a tiny scratch near its top, and it was still dying. Even so, it did have one new feature. In its center it held a new impression: the shape of Ian.

He stared at it, and an energy pulsated from the tips of his fingers to the bottoms of his toes. He saw its ugliness, its age, its wear, its time, and its loss, but now his heart told him a fresh story. He had discovered something special.

He sat down and received a tiny bounce in return. He placed his palm on top of the mattress and pushed softly. He breathed in still air, filled his lungs with generous oxygen, and breathed out his carbon waste. In that moment, all things had become clear: His life was motionless, lethargic, and aimless, but in the dreams all was endless, awake, and stunning. Each dream had delivered a faint caress of something he had been missing. Maybe a sensation, maybe a spectacle, Ian wasn't quite sure. Yet he couldn't help but find himself infatuated with the dreamers' stories.

Regi had cried to his mother in a flash of dazzling light and begged in an infinite church.

Lizzy had been dragged into an ocean by a stone and watched a city rise from grass.

Adriana had experienced panic, fear, and joy. She had

forgotten the name of her brother and the face of her father, but she had also laughed on the river.

He knew they weren't even born as his dreams. Instead, he saw through the dreamers in reverse order—first Regi, then Lizzy, and finally Adriana. They had forged liquid alloys of dream, memory-emotion, in the molten environment of their nighttime subconsciouses, and then bled them out into his mattress, preserving them for another tomorrow.

And now their old dreams were leaking out.

Ian smiled. Finally he had something to find, something to do, a reason to be. He would find her: the woman by the water, the screamer, the smiler, Adriana. He would find her, she would tell him her story, she would explain her dreams.

But that could come later, he decided.

He jumped, and in a blaze of reckless excitement, pulled out his phone and messaged Hallie: *You want to grab those drinks?*

Staring at the screen, he waited, feeling his adrenaline slowly drain from his body. His chest scolded him for running up the stairs. He lay down on his bed and stretched his legs and waited for his body to stop hurting. Then he closed his eyes and nearly fell asleep, until his phone buzzed.

He jumped back up, reached for the small black portal, and saw it was a call from Hallie. He hesitated, then moved in.

"Hello?"

"Hi, are you sure you want to go out tonight? I thought you work like nine to seven?"

Ian realized she was right. He didn't care. "It's fine. I just want to hang out."

"Cool. I'm going out with some friends tonight. We're going to the Bay. I'll send you the address."

At 8:25 p.m., colors burst across a long glass pane. The Bay was a medium-end bar dressed up as a high-end bar, stuck at the end of a busy block full of wandering tourists, old men with backs bent low, and women who violently swung their bags as they hustled to their next destination. Ian checked the map on his phone to make sure it was the right spot. The screen's brightness cut through the darkness of the evening and revealed its truth: the bar in front of him with the sign "The Bay" was, indeed, the Bay.

Walking toward the bar's entrance, he gazed into its long window. Inside was a dark room with soft lights, young people, and soon-to-be-forgotten conversations, each fluttering among one another.

He reached the entrance and approached a large man wrapped in a puffed-up coat. In the evening's haze, he could not fully see the bouncer's eyes, nor his face. By the middle of winter, everyone in the City had become absorbed by the night, just to different extents. After he received a grunt, he slipped into the Bay, pulled his hands out of his pockets, and rubbed them together, searching for warm blood.

Throughout the bar was the quiet murmur of sparse patrons. A couple sat on colorful armchairs to Ian's right, and across the floor, a forty-some-year-old man sipped on his drink. He took it slowly, letting every drop drip into his mouth, and after he was finished, he took his foot and spun the stool he sat on.

Ian watched him circle around the bar. The man first examined the couple whispering in the corner, then the college boys arguing over pints, until he reached Ian. His chair stopped perfectly across from him, and the two briefly made eye contact. The man had a bright-blue gaze that cut through the dimness of the bar, with eyes that hissed tiredness, boredom, loneliness. He had lived—was still living—a confused life that had led him there, to that night, to that moment. It was all painted so clearly on his face that Ian had no choice but to take it in and absorb a sliver of an entire life in one glance, absorb the weight of his living. It was impossible to look away as a raw coolness ran through Ian's heart. *What is his story?*

However, after that brief moment, the man pushed his foot against the floor and swiveled himself back around. They would never see each other's faces again, and despite being only ten feet away, he was gone forever.

Ian sat at an empty black table and pulled out his phone to kill some time. As he stared at the screen, he could hear people shuffle in, but he did not look up. He scrolled and scrolled, searching and searching across endless seas of content and distractions, until he heard, "Hi, Ian."

Dragged from his digital universe, he shut off the device and jerked his head up. In front of him stood Hallie, along with two strangers by her side. One was a tall, wiry young Asian man with a round face and a weak beard, and the other was a short young white woman with a strong chin and a feverish energy.

Suddenly, the three of them were sitting around him. Ian tightened up, crossing his legs and holding his hands in his lap.

"This is John and Katie," Hallie said.

"Hi," Katie said.

"Nice to meet you," John said.

"Good to meet you too," said Ian.

Ian didn't know what to make of them. John had half his head shaved and the other half slicked back and wore an earring in one ear, while Katie wore thick black mascara and a sneaky smile.

"How do you guys know each other?" asked Ian.

"We met in a class," John said, and just after he sat down, he stood up. "I'm going to get a drink. You all interested?"

Katie was the next to hop up, and then Hallie slowly followed. Ian could feel the Sunday blues creeping down his spine, but as he watched the three strangers walk away, he decided to see if he could forget them for one weekend. He rose and followed them into the fray.

"So you guys met on a subway?" John yelled.

"Yeah," said Ian, "we met on the subway."

"I see." John took another sip of his drink. He had six down. He originally had said he wanted to stop at four, but on his fifth, he grinned, declared, "YOLO," and took it all at once.

Ian had swallowed two and could already feel the weight of the late night. He was out of practice, and his eyes burned from the lights in the dark, and his ears stung against the electronic music, but he ignored the pain. He instead opted to sneak glances at Hallie, sip more, and sink deeper into his own head.

Katie inched closer to the table. "I'm not a big subway fan. Last week I saw a rat and its baby crawl out of a hole. They were both as big as my arm, seriously. They tried to grab the trash someone had thrown on the tracks, but then Mama Rat hit the electric rail and went zap! And it was all over."

Ian made a face, and John started laughing.

"Honest to god, I'm not kidding. They were as big as my head," Katie said.

"Really? That's crazy!" John exclaimed. "I feel like I might've seen that in a video or something."

Katie waved and laughed. "It might've been from a video. I can't remember."

"What happened to the baby rat?" asked Ian.

She sipped her drink and said flatly, "It went back into the hole."

"Anything can happen here," Hallie said. "That's for sure."

As the Bay grew louder with the growing crowd, the group's conversation grew slower. After a stretched moment of silence, John stood up again. He made an awkward gesture toward the bathroom, and Katie stood up as well to follow him. Halfway across the dance floor, he motioned for Hallie to join them, but she waved him off. John shrugged his shoulders, and he and Katie disappeared down a corridor.

Ian stared on as they left. "What was that about?"

Hallie looked toward the corridor. "They have some bad habits."

"What does that mean?"

Hallie turned to him and held her index finger under her nose and snorted in stale air.

"Oh," said Ian. He paused before he asked, "What about you?"

Hallie propped her arm on the table and rested her head against a loose fist. "No, I don't mess with that kind of stuff. Alcohol's more than enough." She looked at him. "I have too much to focus on."

The two sat in silence until Hallie squinted at Ian. "So what's your story? What are you about? Why did you move here?"

"What do you mean?"

"I didn't think it was that hard of a question," she said. "I asked, 'Why did you move here?'"

Ian looked outside the bar's windows, and the dark streets of the City looked back at him. He shifted in his chair. "Why does anyone move anywhere? I found a job. It was convenient."

Hallie peered at him before straightening her neck and leaning back in her chair. "That's a weak reason."

Ian frowned. "What about you then? Why did you come here?"

Hallie tapped the side of her cheek, then faced him head on. She always did that, he had noticed, looked him straight on. He adored it and despised it; her intensity was disarming. "I needed something new," she said. "My family has a nice house, but I couldn't live in suburbia forever. I like the energy here."

"You don't miss the grass?"

Hallie, distracted by the crowd, didn't respond.

"Come on, let's dance." She grabbed Ian's hand and pulled him up. As he followed her into the chaos, he noticed how soft her palm was.

Ian was not much of a dancer, but as he watched Hallie move to the rhythm, his brain told his body there was enough alcohol in his blood to at least try to dance. He moved close to her and wondered what she was looking for.

Here she was, the commuter, the biker, the artist, and she was looking to him. He thought about how all of his prior relationships had stalled out. In each one, it seemed both parties ended up just not caring enough for things to continue. Or maybe it was just him; he couldn't tell, not through the vodka. Though none of that really mattered. Looking at her, in the late hours of a cold night, it all didn't matter. He forgot everything that had happened, and everything that would happen, and instead just moved.

Gradually, the beat grew badder, the heat grew hotter, and the two grew tighter. Ian looked into her eyes and wanted to say something, but no words came out. It didn't matter. She wrapped her hands behind his neck and kissed him.

For a brief moment, destined to become lost to time, destined to fade in a vast universe, it was just the two of them, alone together in the crowd. Ian had no thoughts rattling in his mind, and his body was loose. Finally, he felt free.

Breaking the moment, Hallie slowly pulled back and gave a foolish smile. "I'm glad I caught you on the train," she shouted.

He nodded. "Me too." And they kissed again.

Time wore on with dancing and holding and kissing, until Ian's exhaustion finally caught up to him. His legs buckled, and despite his excitement, his head was beginning to dip. He

pulled back and pulled out his phone to check the time.
1:12 a.m.

His eyes widened and, slurring his words, he said, "I need
to go... I need to go to sleep. I have a presentation tomorrow."

Hallie nodded. "Okay." She looked at him and waited.

"Okay. Well, then, I'll catch you later," said Ian.

She began to turn away and approach her friends when
Ian said, "Wait." She turned back to him. "Do you want to
come to a wedding with me?"

Hallie smiled. "Seems a little serious. Maybe. Just text me
the details." Then she disappeared into the chaotic blob of
bodies.

IAN ROLLED ONTO HIS BACK. Tomorrow would be an early day,
but he was restless. His body was still electrified and his
thoughts were tugged between what could be and what was.
He had managed to subdue them for the last half hour by
scrolling on his phone, but now, trying to sleep again, they had
boiled back to the surface. He squirmed and squirmed but
found no relief.

He wanted to see Hallie again, her eyes, her soft skin. He
wanted to see her soon. Then, mentally hopping through the
events of the day, Ian realized he hadn't even thought about
the dreams since he'd seen her. How could he not think about
them? Everything was so close to a breakthrough; he could
feel it.

He imagined where Adriana could be that very moment.
He tried to visualize her watching the river run and leaning
back in a white chair, while she breathed in hot, dry air. The
scene brought him a temporary reprieve, and he so desperately
wanted to be there, but quickly his weak and frenetic imagination failed him.

Instead his mind delivered him an unexpected memory, a

memory of his mother's mother. A memory of how she would always fall asleep in a lazy white wooden chair in his parents' backyard within the first ten minutes of sitting down. As a boy he would stare up at her, contemplating if he should wake her and tell her the food was ready. Glimpses of all the stories she would tell from that chair played in his head, and for an infinitesimal moment, his memory took him back there, back as a boy with her on the grass. He could see her so clearly, so vividly, until he dismissed the thought.

It was an ancient memory. She was four years dead.

In order to find sleep, Ian returned to the dreams. He listened to Regi, watched Lizzy from afar, and experienced Adriana shake the earth. He breathed them in until they occupied every corner of his mind, and only then did he finally find the peace he wanted most of all: slumber.

The room was dark, but the moonlight helped Ian discern the man on the bed. He was sleeping splayed out, with amber-colored arms stretched wide across his mattress. He was exposed too, wearing only boxers and a hairy chest to protect him from the open air. In the dark, he glistened; the film of sweat that coated him from head to toe blended with the little light that had snuck into the room. And next to him was a lump, which had sucked the blanket away from him.

Ian inched closer to the bed to see what was underneath the blanket. Then he shivered and jumped back.

Bright-green rays pierced through the dark and shot directly at Ian. The man had opened his eyes. Captivated, Ian stared deeply into his green irises as he tried to piece together the night's riddle.

Then the man looked away. Leaning over the lump, he tapped the blanket twice and whispered, "Belle, are you awake?"

After a single word, Ian knew instantly. He knew the voice, a voice imbued with smooth dry clay and raw laughter. It rang true, free from any artificial weight, free from false living, free from steel.

Ian saw through the room's dimness and saw the man for who he really was. The man on the bed was no man at all, just an aged boy, a boy who had traveled far from the bank of an old river.

Javi.

Javi gently pulled part of the blanket aside, revealing its secret underneath: the blonde woman from Adriana's dreams. *The blonde. Belle.* Her pale white back had turned to a soft gray in the dark.

Gazing at her, Javi moved closer. "Belle," he whispered, "are you awake? What did you give me?"

Ian's thigh rippled. A sudden wooziness and elation spread through his body, like he hadn't noticed he was at sea and a ship was boldly carrying him above the waves. His legs began to numb, so he leaned against the nearest wall and allowed his body to sink into its hard surface.

"Belle," Javi asked, "do you feel this?" He moved his left hand to touch her back. His index finger connected with her shoulder blade, and that was when the sensation bloomed.

Both Ian and Javi lifted their left hands. They examined them, wide-eyed and mesmerized. The tip of their pointer fingers, where Javi's skin had met Belle's, tingled.

"Belle, wake up. I think something great's happening."

She did not stir and instead continued to sleep under the blanket.

Carefully, Javi leaned over and pulled the blanket off her head. Her hair, a messy, dirty blonde, lay snarled and twisted all over her face and down her body. Javi went over and whispered to her, but Ian had become too distracted to listen.

Her back had transformed. The tiny spot where Javi had touched her had begun to shine like a star born on a dark sky. The spot oozed, and her thin skin underneath the spot festered, shriveling like paper consumed by a fire, until it stopped moving entirely. In its place, a liquid light, an illuminating bright-white sludge, began to slowly drip down her back and burn more of her skin away, replacing it with shine.

Javi, distracted by the feeling in his hand, said, "Belle… you should wake up."

He touched her thin shoulder and softly pulled her closer to him. Sudden ecstasy ran through Ian's hand and into his veins. His forearm had never been more relaxed, and the calm spread down into his leg. His limbs softened, became fragile. He shoved himself against the wall of the room to prevent himself from collapsing. At the same time, Javi pulled his hand back toward his body, launching tiny particles of the liquid light into the air.

Javi examined his own body with glee, while the skin on Belle's shoulder began to twist, snarl, and burn away. It warped, opening and bending, all before disintegrating.

The liquid began to gush. It dripped down her body and seeped into the blanket, filling the bed and the room with light. In a matter of moments, Ian could make out exposed sinew on Belle's shoulder in the shape of Javi's touch, but throughout the process, she remained still with her eyes closed.

Ian's head warmed and his vision blurred. He wanted to fall. His heart was slowing, he could feel it, and his brain was growing quieter. Gravity pulled on him, pulled him into the floor.

Javi kept his grin. He lay on his back and waited for his body to calm down. Movement had become an impossibility. "Belle," he mumbled, "what's in this stuff?"

All the while his sweat had grown into a puddle. It filled the area around his body and mixed with the growing pool of light that had spilled off Belle.

Her open wounds had spread throughout her body, engulfing it. The slow blaze had passed across her sides, up her neck, and down her legs. The skin under her chin had become lost, and the process had climbed between her lips. Finally, it finished pouring over her eyes, and she was no more.

Her body had transformed from a simple corpse of muscle and blood to a faint glow. Her every cell was gone, replaced by a bright glitz. She had become a mysterious beacon in the dark of the night, one with no face or features, only a shell of luster and gleam, shine without substance. Both Javi and Ian stared at her, mesmerized, for she had become whatever Javi wanted to see in her, and nothing that she had been.

Javi's eyes glazed over, and his mouth hung open. He dipped his head on to the bed and Ian began to stumble too, then he fell to the floor.

He couldn't get up, and he knew he would never be able to. Everything was dragging down. Gravity had collapsed into the single room, and all three of them were going to go down. They were to go deep down, down to a darkness he had never seen before in dream or wakefulness, but it did not matter, for the light would guide them.

He could feel the heat Javi felt from the fountain of light. The substance, the lit sludge, had poured over, spilled over everything, and had begun to congeal. Ian closed his eyes and embraced the heat, the fall, the dark. It was easy being so soothed. Accepting the fall felt so much better than fighting it. Consumed by the pleasure, both Ian and Javi could barely sense something was off in their perfect moment of blindness.

That was when Ian heard the gurgle.

Ian's eyes shot open, and he witnessed the liquid light sputtering out of Javi's open mouth. Javi spat, bounced up and down on the bed, and shook. He unleashed a primitive sound, a choke mixed with a guttural cough.

Ian took a deep breath and used his soft arm to prop himself up so he could see him better.

Javi's eyes had grown wide. He nudged his head toward

Belle's light, trying to stretch his incapacitated arm while the rest of his body remained glued to the bed, but his effort did not help; her light continued to flood over and fill his lungs.

He gave an empty gasp and snapped back to his mattress.

In an instant, everything vanished except Ian and Javi. The two of them fell at breakneck speeds. They collapsed down together, down through the void. Ian turned toward Javi. His momentary panic was gone. His eyes were closed and his face had calmed.

Javi knew what Ian had seen in every dream. It was clear on his face. This was it, and all there would be. The two drifted down for one eternity into the next, all of it folding to a close. The sound of the train arrived quietly and faded quickly.

Eventually, Ian realized Javi was no longer with him. He had dissolved into the darkness. Ian was alone.

CHAPTER NINE

Ian sat straight up and dove for his phone.

He searched: *Adriana.* The oracle offered him 415 million results.

Javi. 63 million.

Belle. 790 million.

Adriana Javi Belle. 1 million.

He abandoned the search and opened his chat with Lizzy. He dragged the screen lower and lower, digging back in time until he found what he was looking for: Lizzy's old address, 34th and 82nd.

He looked up the apartment complex online and found an ugly old website with a phone number etched in its corner. With shaking hands, he tapped in the digits. One by one, they went in. One by one, he was closer to finding them.

Call.

The phone rang, rattling shrilly into the morning quiet. Ian tried to listen to the continuous ring, but he couldn't process it. His heartbeats bellowed throughout the room, filling his ears, conquering his focus, until he was finally snapped out of his spell when he heard, "*—a message after the beep.*"

BEEP!

Ian, tongue-tied, sputtered, "I-I need… I need the number of someone who lived here. Adriana. Her name is Adriana." He pulled the phone down, glanced at the time, and ended the call.

It was 5:22 a.m.

Everything pulsated. His body heaved and his spine was wired. He could not unsee the images, nor could his muscles forget the electric sensations. He needed clarity. He needed to find her, then he could find all of them—Adriana, Javi, and Belle. They would tell him what he had seen. They would tell him why he had been chosen to be their dreams' keeper. They would help him understand everything.

He shivered in his bed, rolled, tossed, and eventually gave up on falling back to sleep. He rose and tiptoed into the shower. Resting his head against the thin wall, he barely felt the warm water fall on his back. He would need to leave soon.

Out the door, his head shook.

Off the train, his shoulders shuddered.

On the street, he shivered.

Then he forced himself to stop. He had arrived.

He paced and swallowed the cold. The cold this early could be good, he decided. It would give his body a needed edge. He'd had, what, three hours of sleep? There was no time to relax; it was time to lock in.

He waited outside his office in the dark, with his hands stuffed in his pockets. It was going to snow soon; he could sense it. Had he ever seen snow? Yes, that one time, when he was too young to remember it.

He wished he could be away. Anywhere else, thinking about anything else. Perhaps by the river, basking in the dusty air, away from it all.

A few minutes later, he spotted them. Rohan, wearing a black suit with a blue tie, waved him down, and soon Zoey emerged out of grim streets, barely visible in the dawn. Then lastly Oscar arrived, exiting the office from its entrance. The four grouped up around a black sedan parked on the side of the street and climbed in. Oscar took the wheel, Zoey the shotgun, and the two boys got the back.

Finally out of the cold, Ian's whole body shuddered before it stopped suddenly. Rohan turned to him and sleepily asked, "You all right?"

In a hushed tone, Ian said, "Yes, I'm fine. It was just cold outside."

They drove in silence out of the City. Ian rested his head against the glass window but couldn't sleep. Invisible wasps buzzed around his brain, stabbing his neurons, keeping him thinking. His eyes registered the trees zooming by and the cars zipping across the road, but he watched something entirely different.

Deep into the journey, Rohan broke the group's silence with a quiet voice. "How were your weekends?"

Disrupted, Ian was relieved that Rohan had at least eased them into sound, but then Zoey went ahead and shattered the quiet. "It was great, fantastic! We got a sitter, and me and the hubby went out and saw a show, and then we caught up with his brother. We hadn't had much 'us' time in a while. How was yours?"

Rohan frowned. "It was all right. I went back home to visit my parents."

"Didn't you go last weekend?" she asked.

Rohan nodded. "I did. My dad's not doing so hot, so I'm going by as much as I can to help out my mom."

"Oh," Zoey said.

The car quickly filled with an awkward and invisible odor. Or at least that was how Ian sensed it.

"I'm sorry," she said.

Rohan waved it off. "Don't be. Things happen."

"Well, you're a good son, spending that much time with them."

"They were good parents." Rohan smiled. "A little pushy. Sometimes very pushy. I can remember this one time I came home after a teacher told them I fell asleep in class. *Ro! Tum kar kya rahe ho?*" he said, then laughed. "They wanted to know what the hell I was up to. They wanted a lot for me and my sister. No doubting that. They asked a lot from us too. They still ask a lot. But you know what? It kind of all worked out." Rohan looked around the car, expecting a response, but nothing else was said. Oscar continued to drive, while Zoey gazed out the window.

With some desperation, Rohan turned to Ian. "How about you?"

Ian was gazing into space when he realized he was being watched. He turned around and looked at Rohan, whose eyes twitched ever so slightly at the sight of Ian's face.

"What?" asked Ian.

"How are your parents?"

"Oh. They're fine, I guess. I don't call much. They're busy with retirement."

"I see," Rohan said. "So how was your weekend?"

Ian turned back to the window and resumed gazing aimlessly, wondering what they would understand. He saw so much, and they saw so little. How could he describe it to them?

Should he say how he was searching for answers to inexplicable questions? Or how desperately he wanted to know everything and how little he did? Or how he had kissed a beautiful girl last night but feared it wouldn't last? Or how little he had slept? Or how little he wanted to be on this trip?

He thought briefly and said, "It was fine. Not much happened."

· · ·

WITH ONE HAND in his pocket, Ian fondled his phone and tapped his foot. His spine hung low, and he breathed with his mouth open. Next to him, Zoey smiled to the crowd of five and said, "We're so very excited to show you the new Paper Now."

Zoey, Rohan, and Ian stood in front of a projection of their final redesign. Before them, two pale executives from Paper Now sat with two other younger men, who furiously took notes in black journals, and next to them was Oscar, whose eyes were laser focused, concentrating on every detail of the meticulous slideshow they had spent weeks preparing for a thirty-minute meeting.

"So as you can see here, we believe the redesign will clean up the user experience, easing the pathway from entry to purchase…"

Zoey smiled at their clients while Ian held a lost gaze, floating in his personal image gallery.

"…Now Rohan will explain how our engineers will change the backend of the site."

Rohan strode forward. "Thanks, Zoey. So we will be integrating…"

Sweltering skin, body burning, light churning.

"…The new platform will help you to delight customers…"

Moonlit midnights, all dead by daylight.

"…Now Ian will explain our renewed checkout process, optimized for capturing customers."

He needed to meet these people. Their dreams were so radiant, so real. First he needed to find Adriana. Lizzy might still know something; she might know where she'd gone.

Oscar's glare was the first signal that told Ian something was wrong.

The man at the head of the table asked, "Yes?"

Everyone and everything was staring at Ian. He was at the core of the earth, and the weight of their eyes shoved him down, compressing all his sides into a tiny ball. If he could have ever said something intelligible, now it truly was impossible. After an eon, he began to open his mouth and managed to get just a hint of a word out when Zoey stepped up.

"So if you follow this line, you can see what the customer will see," she said.

Oscar's and Ian's eyes met. Ian could feel a single bead of cold sweat dripping down from his armpit, rolling down his shirt, and sticking to his body. Slowly, Oscar wrote on his yellow pad.

Oh, what the hell is he writing on his yellow pad?

His chest tightened. He wanted to be anywhere but there, anywhere but trapped in those four walls.

"…We really hope you're as excited about the redesign as we are. Please let us know if you have any questions."

Ian's tension moved down to his heart as he adjusted himself to face the two executives straight on, readying for a barrage. Instead they glanced at each other and their other two men. Then the one on the left straightened himself in his chair and spoke.

"I think it's great."

"Yes, I agree," the other said. "I think it's really good."

The first added, "Maybe you could look into keeping the old colors the same. It might cause less confusion."

Ian sighed, Zoey smiled, and Rohan let out a slight chuckle, and then eventually swallowed it. After a pause, Oscar said, "We can do that."

The first man stood up and said, "Great. Well, have your guys call our guys and send the sucker over. Good job. We got to run. Thanks again." He walked out, and like a pack of ducklings, each of the other men followed him out of the room.

After the door closed, the team looked at each other and said nothing. Zoey pulled out the cord connecting her laptop to the screen, while Rohan tiptoed toward the exit. Ian stood still, staring at the floor.

Oscar continued to sit and review his notes. "Hey, guys," he said, "listen to me for a second."

He was examining his yellow pad and then suddenly looked up.

"First of all, good job. They seemed to like it... I have some comments." He looked down and began to read, "On your second slide, there was too much talking going on; no one could concentrate. Later on, you should've had something in your back pocket to engage the clients more... A wow factor, a hypothetical, a detailed example... they were getting bored."

Then he looked back up and paused for a moment. Ian spotted a bulging vein in his neck. "And I just have to ask: what the hell were you laughing about, Rohan?"

The room became dead silent.

"Seriously, what was so funny? Can anyone tell me?"

Everyone looked down except Rohan, who met him straight on.

"Fine. Don't tell me. Just don't act like that in front of a client again. It's sloppy." Then he turned to face Ian. "Ian, you stay here for a second. Everyone else get out."

Zoey and Rohan snatched up their things and hustled out of the room. Oscar waited for the door to slowly drift to a close before he opened his hands in exasperation.

"Dude? What was that about?"

Ian took a second, combing over his words. His spine had depressurized, weakened and loosened and melted, but at least any anxiety had left his body. All that lingered was a dull sense of shame.

"I was distracted."

Oscar shook his head. "Distracted by what?"

"I guess I just zoned out."

Oscar jumped up and snapped, "Did you practice the presentation?"

Ian nodded. "We practiced as a group a few days ago."

"I just don't get it." Oscar walked to the door and opened it. He shook his head. "Don't do that again. Wake up." He slammed the door behind him.

Then he opened it again. "Come on, we need to get back to the city." Then he closed it again.

Ian stood alone, staring at the floor. He inched toward the door, involuntarily yawned, and grabbed onto the closest chair to catch himself. He had lost balance; he was too tired to stand.

With his head dipped down, he reached into his pocket, pulled out his phone, and searched for missed calls. There were none.

He found and tapped the number of Lizzy's old apartment complex. The phone rang, but there was no answer.

B elle was draped in a light-brown dress made of wool sheared from sheep born in far-off lands. It hugged her body loosely and softly as she stood in front of a mirror and analyzed herself, examining every angle and curve. Her skin tone melted seamlessly with the fabric, as she had turned her white husk into an athletic brown, baked by the sun and perfected by the beach. Even her hair carried a vitality of its own, dripping bright blonde gold down her exposed back.

Under the bright florescent light, she seemed to shimmer. But Ian did not look at her for long; rather, he looked to the floor. On the floor, she was caught and blurred by the shine of clear marble tiles. He watched her reflection move like a puddle of dirty light.

They were in a clothing store and traffic was slow, with only a few other shoppers hidden away, quietly perusing deals on back alley shelves and racks. And in the middle of the store, in the middle of her dream world, was her.

In front of their mirror, Belle and Mirror Belle paced, turning their bodies, inspecting every inch. Ian could tell by the way they stroked the fabric and by the way they smirked at one another that they were satisfied, extremely satisfied. In fact, it was the greatest dress she had ever seen, and she felt the greatest she had ever been. Ian could feel it too, a euphoria that streamed throughout his blood, making both their bodies light, nearly floating above the ground.

Next to them, another woman materialized. She wore a blank name tag attached to a white blouse and fitted dark-blue jeans.

Belle turned to her and grinned. "I love it. It's beautiful."

The woman smiled and nodded. "It looks great. Do you want me to ring it up?"

"Yes!"

The two moved a few feet, and there appeared a perfectly rectangular counter Ian had not noticed before. Nor had he noticed the stunning image. High above the counter, resting on the back wall, was a massive framed photograph.

On it, a nameless model ran on a beach, her feet sinking into the white sand while she flashed a brilliant smile and wore a short summer dress which breezed against an invisible gust. Everything about the shot was pristine: the air, the water, the sand, her smile, the sun. Indeed, her frozen image was a preservative of perfection, and her picture filled Ian and Belle with a raw thrill.

He glanced back at Belle. She had changed—now she wore shorts and a crop top, and she held the brown dress in her hands.

The cashier scanned the dress, and Belle handed her a plastic card. The woman swiped it, the two waited for a moment, and a moment again.

BUZZ.

Ian grabbed his ears and winced. The rejection was loud and shrill enough that the machine may as well have cursed at them. All at once, the euphoria that had fueled them evaporated as quickly as it came, leaving behind a small nervous pang.

The cashier shook her head. "The card's been denied."

Belle leaned forward, getting closer to the cashier's face. "What?"

"The card's been denied. It didn't work."

"I don't think you should get that one."

Ian and Belle turned to the new voice. A shorter, older woman stood next to them. She wore big round designer sunglasses, and golden bracelets dangled on her arm. Her face was strangely tight, like it had been stitched together by a needle, and her makeup was loud.

"I don't like that dress," the woman said.

"Why not?" Belle muttered.

"It didn't look good. The color doesn't suit you. Neither did the fabric, too cheap, too low quality. We'll find another one that'll look much better on you."

Belle shook her head. "No, I really liked it. I don't want another one. I like this one."

The woman walked back into the center of the store and waved Belle on. "Come, come. I'll show you."

Belle meandered along, following her back into the store's maze. "Mom, I don't want a different dress."

Mom stopped and slowly turned around. She took off her glasses and coldly stared at her daughter. Ian hesitated, expecting a conflict to erupt, but then she suddenly smiled.

"You should really try this one. It's very chic, made out of silk." In her wrinkled hands, she presented a sleek royal-purple dress. She handed it to her daughter, who reluctantly rubbed it in her hands and held it close to her chest.

"Remember this," her mother said. "Good women wear something nice. You don't want to be a little girl, wearing ripped jeans and brown jackets forever."

Belle's eyes widened. "Oh," she said. Belle sat on the floor and laid the purple dress over her body. She stared blankly into the space around her. "I guess I just never knew what to wear."

Instantly, Ian sensed something tremble in the bottom of his stomach, and his body grew heavier. Then, without hesitation, despair burst out. Belle started crying slowly, then quickly. Tears streamed down her face, forming a puddle around her, accumulating without hesitation, spotting the side of her body. Simultaneously, Ian also found a few droplets slide down his face before he rubbed them away. This wasn't his dream, he reminded himself. As he watched her shudder and her sobbing began to overflow, he experienced a sensation unique to him. He pitied her.

He stepped up to try to comfort her, despite knowing he would fail, until he caught a whiff of something. He took another sniff and another... and another, then retreated.

There was this... *smell*. A rancid, horrible, foul smell. A smell that doused the air and spread throughout the store, like some kind of disease.

There was no smell quite like it. In fact, the remarkable odor delivered to Ian faint crumbs of memories, repressed times of being nine and nineteen. They came back suddenly and simultaneously: experiences of being a child, dizzy off the bus, and experiences of being a young man, dizzy off the booze. They both had resulted in the same outcome. Ian took one last sniff, just for a final confirmation, and indeed confirmed it. Vomit.

Belle continued to cry, until her entire side became covered in a splatter of stinky tears. Ian looked up and saw Mom was long gone, and the clerk, the store, and other customers were also missing. All that remained was Belle curled above an invisible floor, crying in the darkness.

Ian scratched the side of his face and wondered what he should make of it all. He wondered why Adriana had feared this sobbing woman so much, and why she sobbed at all.

Trying to avoid the smell, he kept his mouth open and his nostrils tight. He continued like that, barely breathing, while he watched her cry with her eyes closed, until he saw something approaching. In the distance, a small silver slug was growing larger. A rumble emerged.

"Is that the damn train again?" he asked aloud.

The train began to accelerate toward the two of them and brought its sound with it. Never before had it felt so close and so certain as it came right at them. Ian expected a quick end, but when he looked at Belle, she remained fastened to the ground, shivering and sobbing. He glanced back at the train and realized it was not going to stop.

He began to run.

He ran into the darkness, into the place beyond sound, but the darkness brought no relief. There was nowhere to go. Rattled, he could hardly stand. His legs, knees, and feet trembled, succumbed to gravity and torsion and emotion. Even if he were quicker, more agile, it would not be enough. No matter how far he tried to go, he found himself next to Belle, while the train simply grew louder and closer. Around them, a subway platform had formed and entrapped them at the bottom of its pit, stuck in the middle of its tracks while the machine advanced.

Frustrated and distracted, he lost his focus and drank in another helping of the rich scent, the smell, the spew, the sweat, the waste. He spat and coughed. Everything was too much. He wanted to scream at her, stomp, do whatever it would take, but when he looked at the poor girl on the ground, he knew it wouldn't do anything. The train was inevitable.

He assessed his options and sighed and spat again. His stomach began to gurgle; it seemed he had fallen ill as well. He lay beside Belle and watched her heave. Her hair had become a mess, frizzy and frayed at the ends, caked with tears. As she whimpered, she cried with her mouth open, and Ian could see flashes of yellowed teeth shaking. She looked completely different than the woman she had stared at in the mirror. Her complexion had been counterfeited, her confidence had collapsed, her vibrance had vanished, and her glow was gone.

She had returned to how she was when he had first met her.

He turned to face the train. It demanded his attention; it had come too close to be ignored any longer. It was milliseconds away, with a blinding light and a shriek that penetrated every inch of his body.

Then it arrived.

When it struck Belle, Ian's heart stopped for a moment.

He fell back and clutched his chest.

His muscles twitched, convulsed, and shuddered. His body alone controlled him for a half-second, a temporary moment of thoughtless drift with a consciousness somewhere lost, until, without even noticing, his mind was back, all movement had stopped, and nothing remained in sight.

CHAPTER TEN

I t didn't seem right to sit on the subway wearing a tuxedo, so Ian offered to pay for a cab.

He had waited three days for her response. For three days, he habitually pulled out his phone to check for a message, even though he knew no reply waited for him. But then, on the third day, he finally saw the light.

The notification blinked at him through the evening's darkness while he lay on his bed, collapsed after work. Her answer brought inspiration and anxiety, all in three words:

Sure, I'll go.

A minute later she followed with: *Sorry for the slow response. I've been busy.*

Now, a few days later, in the backseat of a taxi, Ian fumbled with his fingers and a carbonated mind, bubbling from multiple streams of life and dream.

They—Ian and the driver—were traveling to their first stop. They were separated by a thick glass divider in the middle of the car, which offered only a narrow hole of communication. Ian didn't mind the barricade. In fact, he enjoyed it. The solitude fit the landscape.

Snow had fallen over the City, quieting loud streets into submission through the awesome cumulative power of tiny ice crystals. It had arrived heavy in the night, all in a rush, packing itself together in a desperate attempt to survive the long haul, despite facing an impossible challenge: the inevitable melt. But since dawn, the fresh snowfall had become a faint trickle, a romantic dusting for a winter wedding.

Ian watched the snow trickle down while he ignored the driver. He didn't need to speak to him; he had learned his whole identity in one glance. Embedded into the car's side was a plastic pane which held his photo and registration. Ian had glanced at it when he first arrived and swallowed the entire life captured in cloudy plastic. His name was Ojo. He had round glasses and a stern expression. And that was who he was, all he needed to be. The driver, Ojo.

Outside cars drifted by, all touched up by the light snow. As they moved throughout the City, block by block, buildings transformed in shape, age, and design, but under the snow they all looked the same. Gray rectangles covered in a shade of white. All so dull compared to the dreams.

Ian checked his phone again. She had sent: *See you in a bit!*

He shut it off and rubbed his head. That morning pain had rung in his ears, throbbing and banging at the same time, creating an endless flow of discomfort. He had guzzled water, desperate to ease it before the big day, but it refused to go away. When he had started walking toward the cab, it had only grown louder. It seemed the cold had inflamed it, lining his disquiet with frost to create a fierce wintery ache.

Soon traffic closed around them and brought the taxi to a halt. He peeked out into the window of the car next to them. Across the lane, he could make out its driver perfectly.

The stranger wore a polo shirt and had fat, puffy cheeks. He drove a thick and heavy white machine, happily drinking modern energy translated from ancient matter. He sat above Ian's taxi, gazing at the road as its general while he stroked his sparse hair and groaned and violently yelled. Ian saw his windows rattle against his voice, as if his shout would shatter the car when he reached his final furious breaking point.

And next to him was a woman. Ian heard her clearly, even though she said nothing; he could see silent words in her eyes. She stared straight ahead toward the road, pretending to look at nothing at all, but really she was listening to everything, letting it swirl inside, before she would lock it away and try to ignore it. Although Ian wanted to know the topic of discussion, he knew the content didn't matter. Her face was enough; it told him more than enough.

Then the light changed. Ian and the driver went straight, the strangers turned right, and both parties became lost to each other forever.

Ian closed his eyes and took a brief moment to rest, imagining himself somewhere else. He shifted his feet and repositioned himself in the back of the cab. No angle was comfortable. The headache was only half the problem. He was awake-exhausted, a blend of too many late nights with early mornings infused with a nervous excitement to see Hallie again. All together, it formed a noxious combination, which the bumps on the roads didn't help.

Along the way, they waited for an old woman who moved slower than time itself, crawling across the street on six legs: two human and four walker wheels.

He tapped his foot. He still had no response from the apartment complex. He still didn't know where Adriana was. He still had no lead. The phone number would be a dead end, he decided. He would go back to Lizzy and ask her at the wedding if she knew where the old woman had moved. She would know something, she must. He had messaged her about her old landlord's contact information, but she had not responded.

A few minutes later, Ian said to the driver, "If you could stop on the right, that would be ideal."

The driver did so, though he probably did not need Ian's direction. She was impossible to miss.

She lit the white and gray slate she stood on. Her dress, deep and blue, splashed color onto the bleak winter day, and her heels elevated her above the ground's grime. Tiny particles of snow and soot had mingled and intertwined before they landed on her hair and dress, painting her as an urban snow angel.

She flagged them down, pulled the door open, stepped in, shoved it closed, slid to the middle seat of the taxi by Ian, and stopped. Then she shivered.

"It's damn cold out there," she said.

Ian nodded and told the driver to go to their next stop. "You look nice."

"Thanks," she said. "I was wondering, whose wedding is this?"

Ian turned to her. "Did I not tell you?"

She shook her head.

"It's my cousin Lizzy's. And her fiancé Regi's."

"Oh." She leaned back and stretched her arms above her head and yawned. "Do we like Regi?"

Ian smiled at her. "I don't know. What kind of question is that?"

"I want to know what kind of wedding this is. Like am I supposed to be happy about it, disgruntled, or is it all about the free food?" She wagged her pointer finger at him. "You've always got to know what kind of wedding it is."

He took a second to respond, trying to process her words in his ailing head. He nervously chuckled. "I would hope one could be happy about most weddings. Regi seems fine. I haven't talked to them much."

"What does he do?"

"You know… I don't really know."

Hallie looked at Ian closer. "How did they meet?"

He realized he had no idea. "I never asked."

She scoffed. "What *do* you know?"

He touched the glass of the window with the back of his hand. The cold infected his nerves, causing his muscles to twitch. He wanted it, he needed that kick, he needed something, anything to keep himself going, to keep him focused, to keep him awake. Already the day was getting too long, too tiring.

"I guess I know a hell of a lot about paper websites."

The drive was thirty minutes uptown, heading to the apex of the City. At some point, as traffic slowed and the car hit a rhythm, the two in the back grew silent. They both stared into the outside world, immersed in their own thoughts, and dug deeper into themselves. Ian didn't know if he should say something or let the quiet stew. The car's slow progression and steady stops and starts had begun to nauseate and drowse him, so he leaned his head against the window for balance. He considered the consequences of disappointing the stranger next to him, but then realized that he had nothing he wanted to say to her, except that her dress reminded him of a dream.

"Almost there."

Ian's head snapped up. He immediately grabbed the phone in his pocket. His eyes moved from side to side as his mind tried to digest an overabundance of stimuli and determine where he was. He had fallen asleep… He was in a taxi… He was still in the taxi. He was with Hallie and the driver. They were going to the wedding.

Ian looked down at his side. Hallie had pushed her finger into his gut to prod him awake. He shook himself out of his shallow sleep, and she said, "I made a new friend."

"Hello!"

He rubbed his eyes and glanced around, taking a moment to recognize whose voice had just boomed through the taxi. Then he turned to the tiny gap in the divider. The driver had escaped his box.

"Oh," said Ian. "How are you doing?"

The driver looked up at his rearview mirror, and for the first time, Ian saw his face in motion. He had a wrinkled smile which folded deep into the sides of his face and black freckles on dark-brown skin.

"I'm great! The snow's starting to clear up. And your friend told me it's wedding time. I love weddings."

Ian glanced back at the picture encased in plastic and then back at the mirror. Despite sharing the same face, the driver and Ojo appeared to be different men.

"Not our wedding," said Ian.

Both Hallie and the driver laughed. "I know that. I'm not deaf, you know," he said. "My daughter got married two years ago, actually."

"Oh, how was it?" Hallie asked.

"It was… okay. Husband's *okay* guy. Well, he a good guy, to be honest. It just was sudden, you know? Didn't feel real, until it was, that's all. So much can change so fast. One day she's my little girl, the next she's married. One day things like *this*, then they like *that*. It's amazing. Just amazing change." He smiled and turned his head to face the tiny gap. "It was a great wedding."

Ian, still trying to wake up, nodded and pretended to listen.

"I think we're almost there," the driver said.

Hallie pointed out the window. "Yes, maybe right there is good."

Outside, under the gentle snowfall, both strangers and distant family had weaved around each other on a clogged street corner. They stood in front of the long gray steps of a mighty church, a stout anomaly against the backdrop of the steely City. As a whole, it was much shorter than the towers that Ian had become accustomed to downtown, but it was robust, solid, and impressive enough to claim its territory and be proud of it. It had a classic feeling, made of gray stone, painted with colored glass, and enchanted by memories.

"Is any of your family coming?"

Ian shook his head. "No. Lizzy's a pretty distant connection. I'm only going because we reconnected. I told them I'd try to see them during Christmas."

Hallie grabbed the car's door handle. "That's good. For me, at least. That would've been a bit awkward." As she opened the door, she looked back toward the gap and said, "Bye, Ojo."

"Bye-bye," he said.

Ian paid, waited a moment, and took off.

They stood on the edge of the crowd, hesitant to crash inside. Regi's family and Lizzy's family had assembled separately, chattering amongst themselves while they took pictures and told stories.

Then the sting of a cold front arrived. A gust attacked the street, blowing through everyone, creating a collective shiver. Instantly the trickle of people entering the church turned into a stream as they ran to escape the wind's bite. The entrance, tall wooden doors, became packed with the two families, pushing and colliding with one another, melding into one. Ian watched it unfold in silence and peeked above them, into the church, until Hallie took his hand and pulled him into the fray.

Only when they entered did Ian experience its true might. Inside, with its high walls and booming acoustics, it hinted at its full power. The pews were smooth mahogany, and its center aisle featured a long wine-red carpet. Most impressive was its back: above the altar was an elaborate window of glass, manipulating white light into fantastic reds, yellows, and greens.

Ian trailed Hallie as he gazed at the glass. They sat down, and he asked, "Isn't this beautiful?"

Hallie looked at him curiously. "That's a little more poetic than what I've come to expect from you."

"Just look at it." He pointed to the light. "It's something special."

"True," Hallie said. "Actually, I had a friend who was into glasswork."

He kept looking ahead. "Oh yeah?"

"Yes, you know how hot it's got to get to make that? You get to 3,000 degrees and can transform sand into glass."

"Oh." He had only heard half the words she said. *3,000 degrees.* His brain was distracted, working, gnawing on something he yearned to understand.

"I think it's pretty amazing what they can do."

He turned to Hallie. He realized he hadn't looked at her close enough since the night they drank, danced, and kissed. Under the wedding's hue, he once again decided that she was beautiful. He wanted to be alone with her. He wanted to hold her soft body against his and tell her everything. How her dress only added to her beauty, how it reminded him of the river of his dreams, and how he wanted to take her with him. He wanted to tell her how he felt. He wanted her to tell him she loved him. And he wanted her to tell him that everything was going to be all right.

But as he opened his mouth to speak, and as she turned face his gaze, his mind offered him a sudden glimpse of an alternate reality. He had ignored it for some time, buried it in the back of his heart, but it escaped in his moment of vulnerability. The visions spilled out in his unfastened emotional gap and attacked all at once.

Regi dipped his head, and the waves devoured Lizzy.

The city emerged, and the room collapsed into cataclysm.

An old man's face melted, and Belle climbed like a zombie from the river.

Light suffocated Javi, and Ian's chest throbbed from impact.

One look at Hallie had brought it all to the forefront. He could see Belle in her eyes; he envisioned the same coming for her. Her skin would fester, burn her away, rip her apart, and reveal her glow, until that too faded. He saw her on the ground, crying, surrounded by a puddle of her tears, smelling of puke. Under the church's lights, he could see it all—old dreams, both beautiful and cruel, all carried away by subway. They reminded him of his ultimate responsibility. His heart carried strangers' weights, and his mind held their truths, and he needed to find resolution.

And with his mind thoroughly clogged, he shuddered.

"Are you okay?"

Are you okay? Hallie's voice rang through the torrent of anxiety and closed the faucet. He inhaled and wiped fresh sweat off his forehead. How easily she had read him. A frustrated heat flashed over him, sending a deep slice of annoyance across his chest. She had been bestowed with a gift of precise perception, automatically concerned and constantly caring. *How fortunate.* Perhaps that was why she was willing to stick to him. She had sensed something wrong with him, and she needed to solve it. He was just getting sick, that was all it was, he assured himself. He was tired and ill and needed some rest.

"Yes, I'm fine. Just a little cold," said Ian.

Waiting for the services to start, he controlled his body with a slow and steady breath. He would speak with Lizzy. She would help him find Adriana, Belle, and Javi, then they would explain what he had seen, what he had felt. They would laugh and cry and tell stories and help him know where he was going, what he should do, and who he should be. And then he would have his peace.

"In this modern and chaotic world, it can often feel as though life is completely uncertain," the officiant began. *"That's precisely why marriage, and specifically this marriage, is a blessing and a beauty…"*

Ian kept his eyes aimed directly forward, trying to ignore the heat coming off of Hallie as they sat scrunched next to each other on the filled pew.

"We will have an exchange of vows, followed by the reception. In the process these two young people will be united and create a lifelong bond." The officiant smiled, flashing abnormally white teeth. *"Reginald and his family have been coming to my church since he was a little boy. It is a personal joy for me to see this moment…"*

It was hot, too hot, in the packed room. The heat came in waves, rolling throughout Ian's body. It birthed in his core, floated up into his brain, and spread throughout his organs. His eyes dipped and his posture slipped. His head had become a dizzy mess, all pointing to one certain need: rest.

The procession had taken forever. Around him, his distant family grinned and laughed and snapped photos as they turned toward the aisle. The moment would be crystallized in their memory forever, but he doubted it would last for him. It would become just another wedding, one of many, marking the beginning of a confused wave of twenty-somethings saying "I do."

Strangers had walked down the aisle, taking so long with every step. One after another, a hodgepodge of humans strolling forward. Ancient grandparents; smiling groomsmen; a best man with a goofy tie; Regi sharp as ever, owning the floor in front of him; delusional bridesmaids; a sophisticated maid of honor; and a tiny boy.

Ian rubbed his hair, remembering Regi's desperation in the night, how much of a frenzy he had been in. Looking at him in this state, it didn't make sense. One night he had been in a panic, now he stood tall and proud. What an actor he must be.

It all was beginning to feel like another uneasy night, another night where he would spend forever searching for a distant sleep, unable to find it. He clenched his jaw until he felt Hallie's light tap his shoulder.

"Wow," she said.

When he looked up, even Ian forgot his discomfort for a moment. Somehow that chaotic curly-haired child had turned into this. He had never considered his cousin to be beautiful, but in front of him was undeniable evidence. When she appeared, she sucked the air out of the room; the crowd forgot they could breathe. Ethereal, she distorted the space around her, becoming a force of her own, pulling all focus onto a singular point: her. Lizzy.

The crowd rose to its feet and Ian followed.

Her dress was voluminous, large enough to swallow her body whole in white satin. It made her every step conquer that much more space. It flowed, gliding behind her. She floated above it all, above everyone.

Ian stared at her hard as she strode down the aisle, and he glanced at Regi. Regi, grinning like a fool, served as her beacon. Then Ian looked back at her.

He had seen this before. This was it. This had been the dream, Regi's dream. He had gazed at the long carpet she walked on. Regi had dreamed this moment... only in dream it had been reversed. She had been walking away, away from him, and he was too weak, too uncertain to tell her to come back and marry him. Now she walked toward him. *What had changed?*

When she had finished her ascent, the spell broke. In a great hustle, the audience jumped at its chance to sit, and Ian collapsed onto the pew with a thump. The heat quickly returned, and everything became inflamed. He could hardly keep his eyes open without nausea churning and growing. He pushed his hands into the hardwood and felt his spine grind against the back of the bench. He glanced to his right. He needed to find a way out.

"When I first saw you walk into the firm I was like, hello there…" Regi began and finished with, *"…I know if she was here, she would love you."*

Ian reexamined both sides. There were five people sitting to his right, eight to his left. They had stacked up around them. Both directions offered no hope of escape. He began to stare at the church's stained glass. He needed something to concentrate on, anything to help him gain some balance.

Hallie tugged on his shoulder and broke his focus. "Unlucky guy," she whispered.

A wave hit. Ian blinked back his nausea. "Yes."

"Regi. You are the sweetest…" Lizzy began.

He needed some water, some rest, anything. He would survive, he told himself, by keeping his head still.

"…I love you so much…"

Just finish the damn speech.

"…Not everything's been easy, but I realized I'd want no one else…"

There was no more time. Ian spoke slowly, finding every word difficult to release. "Hallie… I'm going to… the bathroom."

"What?"

He examined the church's glass windows one last time. Its light had not changed at all since they had arrived. Each panel always gave off the same brightness, the same colors, the same hue. He had seen their truth; it was barely visible, but clear when spotted. There were tiny bulbs on the back of each glass pane, providing a constant artificial light. In the modern world, they didn't need the sun at all.

"Now you may kiss the bride."

He jumped during the second between when Regi and Lizzy moved toward one another and when onlookers stood, clapped, and recorded the moment with their phones. Time froze into a concentrated dose for Ian, and then happened all at once.

He launched his body toward his right. He managed to dodge the first three of them. The second to last woman was *sizable*. She was standing, blocking his way entirely. No options. Ian, on an unstoppable path, moved his foot forward and kneed her, *gently*, on the side of her leg. She plopped down onto the pew. Her husband to her right looked outraged but said nothing and backed up. Ian snuck past him and finally had the momentum he would need. He ducked his body low and didn't look back. He shuffled down the middle aisle, taking long strides. There was no time for anything else. His body was churning. He shoved himself forward and forward and forward, out into the hall. There was the door. He thrust his weight onto it and rolled out onto the street. The wind hit hard. It slammed the door behind him, almost pushed him back, and punched him in the gut. It was now or never. He jumped down from the entrance step and rotated his body to make the wind face his back. Then he opened his mouth, and his vomit was carried out by the wind.

It spilled all over the snowy concrete.

Stumbling back, he looked down. The puke had splattered in front of the church and lined its entrance. And he had gotten bits of breakfast on his shoes. Then he puked again.

Groaning, he lifted his head and searched for witnesses. *There*. Across the street, a boy had stopped to stare at him, mesmerized by the strange vomiter on the cold winter day. Ian glared at him until the two made eye contact. Slowly the boy turned, keeping his eyes fixated on the vomit on the ground as long as he could, before he forced himself to walk away.

Ian bent over the mess in front of him. It rested above the snow as a cocktail of green and brown chunks and goo. What had once been a part of him had become his waste. And now it stared back at him.

He turned to the sky and stretched his neck. He could taste the smell in his throat. He tried to breathe it out, but it didn't help. It was cold enough that his every breath condensed into a fog, and somewhere in that smoke, he knew, were particles of puke. He leaned down and spat on the ground.

Trying to wipe off the puke, he desperately rubbed his shoes against the steps and kicked loose snow over the waste. He was met with middling results; the vomit was hot off the press and worked earnestly to cut through the snow. In meek desperation, Ian walked toward a parked car and grabbed a handful of snow off the top of its hood. He pressed it into a ball and threw it above the mess. It fell and awkwardly sat in the middle of the bile, warming slowly.

With his hands in his pockets, he walked down the street and leaned against the church's wall. His head felt a little better, but he didn't know what to do. He couldn't go back in the church and risk opening the door again, alerting everyone, nor did he want to wait around and be discovered as the puke's perpetrator. So he scanned the street and began to walk. He turned the corner and hid there, occasionally peeking out to see if anyone had left the church.

Then he fumbled with his phone. Its aluminum back and front glass were freezing, like twin icicles cutting into his fingers, but with a shaky hand he managed to send a message to Hallie: *Sorry. Got sick. I'll meet you outside.*

Checking again, he poked his head around the corner and saw the church's doors had opened. One by one, the guests slowly trickled out and moved around the vomit, forming a parted sea, all desperate to avoid the slushy winter stew at the bottom of the stairs. They climbed into their taxis and cars and departed; it was time for the reception.

Ian waited until Hallie finally appeared. She spotted the puke and skipped around it, on the edge of the steps. She wandered halfway down the street, looking around, before she stopped. He exhaled, then approached her. She greeted him with a face mixed with curiosity and concern.

"So that was you?"

He looked back at his vomit and nodded.

Hallie glanced above him, toward the sky, and then back at him with a grin. "The ceremony wasn't that bad."

He managed a faint smile. "Did anyone notice me run out?"

"No, I don't think so. Well, I did because I watched you instead of the kiss. And maybe the woman you tackled." Hallie pointed to her eyes with two fingers and then pointed them back at Ian. "She gave me a death stare, just like that."

He leaned against the side of the church and let his body slump into the stone. "Maybe I should go home."

She nodded. "Probably a good idea. Stay off that wedding food."

"What will you do?"

Hallie took a moment before she said, "I think I'll go to the reception, grab some lunch, and get gone."

"Really?" Ian raised his voice. "You're still going to the reception?"

"Yeah, why not?" She shrugged. "I cleared my schedule for this."

He said nothing. He only stared at the ground in front of him. His head had cleared, but he still had trouble looking at her.

"Well, see you, then," she said.

"Yeah, see you."

She walked to the edge of the street and raised her hand to

call for a cabdriver. As a taxi came to a stop, she turned to Ian. "Don't worry about it. Everyone pukes. I probably puked last week." Then she climbed in, waved goodbye, and was gone.

Ian watched and waited as she rode off. Feeling a new kind of sickness in his stomach, he limped back around the corner and walked to the end of the street. There he pulled out his phone to summon a car with a driver.

The sun shined hard onto Javi, brightening his yellow hardhat, making his arms drip with sweat. He wore ripped jeans and a brown jacket.

Ian approached him and the men around him. They sat on a bench in a construction yard with tools strewn around: jackhammers, drills, and a great claw machine ready to plow the earth.

The workers were a mixed bunch, some young, some old, some with dark skin, some with light, but they all sat with the same flat look across their face. Under the hot sun, it was not a time for talk but for reloading, time to let the day drift by in silence and stare at their jumble of wood, dirt, and cement. Of the group, only Javi showed a hint of emotion, holding a whisper of a smile. Meanwhile, in the distance behind them, the City glittered. They had been tasked with expanding its glory.

Ian stepped aside as a man walked up from behind him. He was short, pale, and held a clipboard. "Okay, boys," he squeaked. "We're going to go up today."

Some of the men on the bench groaned, others nodded

slowly, and Javi rose first. He grabbed a saw from the ground and began.

Work started slowly. Javi and a coworker would pick up a flat slice of wood and move it onto a cutting board. Then Javi cut planks out of it and placed them on the ground. Cutting plank after plank, he thrust his back into it, until he had gathered a small pile of wooden steps.

Meanwhile, the other men found metal poles and beams, which they shoved into the ground. All the while, they did not speak. The only sounds present were distant cars, the saw, wood, earth, metal, friction, and grunts.

Javi grabbed the pile and walked toward the pipes. He crouched and carefully laid a plank above the metal support and then stepped onto it. He repeated this process, and soon he stood on the third step of an infant staircase. Gingerly, Ian followed him, and that was when the work began to spiral.

They were like a machine, accelerating at an unbelievable rate. The men appeared to keep their normal pace, begrudgingly building out the supports while Javi methodically laid out a plank, slowly moving one step higher at a time, but before too long, both him and Ian were gone, high up in the air.

Ian looked around and trembled. Without even noticing, the ground had become a distant sight, the buildings tiny miniatures, and the people barely dots. They had left it all behind.

His heart quivered, fear flowing into his muscles. His core shook, his legs wobbled, and his mind screamed at him. *I am going to fall.* He crouched on the staircase, curled himself, and clutched the step before him. He could not go any higher, *he could not,* he told himself.

But looking up, he saw Javi in front of him. The man, bright under the close sun, simply wiped the sweat off his brow, took a breath, and picked up the next plank. He was on his knees, scraping them against each rough wooden step while he prepared the next one. Fully engrossed, he looked only straight and proceeded without hesitation. He was rising quickly, getting farther away with every passing second. Ian decided the only way forward was with him.

They continued to rise up, up, and up. They passed the clouds, the stratosphere, and finally, the Earth. Ian did not know if they had been walking for a century or an instant. A warm darkness wrapped around them, as the blue sky had faded from view. So far above the earth even the oceans appeared to be simple ponds. Then at last, Javi slowed down. He placed his last step and stood up straight. He stretched his back and raised his arms in triumph and gazed down. Then he jumped.

Shocked, Ian clambered up to the final step and desperately searched below, expecting to see doom.

But there was no disaster, no end, no doom. Instead, Ian's eyes widened. He had discovered something profound; he had realized the true nature of Javi's work. They had gone beyond the ground, beyond the City, beyond the seas, beyond the Earth, and ventured into the near beyond. Javi had built a staircase to the Moon.

Floating gently down, Javi landed softly on the silver rock, sat on his bottom, stretched out his legs, and exhaled, satisfied. Now without a worry and feeling similarly relaxed, Ian jumped. He followed Javi down while being unable to look away from the wonder.

Smiling, Javi watched the Earth spin. He turned his head and shouted, "Baby, you see this?"

On the desolate surface of the Moon, Belle appeared. She walked toward Javi, looking alive, illuminated, moving with grace as her skin carried a faint glow. She sat beside him and rubbed her body next to his.

"It's okay," she said. "Honestly, I would've preferred you guys to finish my patio first."

Javi laughed and pointed to the giant staircase. "Look at that! It's great, right? Don't you think so?"

Belle shrugged. "Like I said, it's okay." Then she grinned. "I know what could make it better." She reached into her pocket and pulled out a small orange jar. She rattled it and twisted its cap open, then extracted a small white pill. "Do you want one?"

Javi shook his head. "Maybe later. I'm fine for now."

"Suit yourself."

She threw the pill into her mouth and gulped it down while Javi watched the blue planet spin slowly. Then she haphazardly pointed down the staircase and murmured, "There's that damn train again."

Standing next to the pair, Ian peered down the staircase. She was right, it was coming.

It began as a small glimmer in the distance, barely making a sound, but soon it grew into a bullet running straight toward them, zooming along its tracks.

Javi let out a mock sigh, continuing to grin. He wrapped his arms around Belle, hugged her tight, and whispered, "Let's never leave this place."

Watching the two of them among the stars, Ian's chest grew warm. They had ascended somewhere far beyond the weights and worries of the Earth, somewhere he could only find in dream. He wanted it to continue forever, he wanted the feeling forever, but he could see the landscape was fading to dust, and he could hear the train growing louder.

The beauty of the moment would disappear, along with everything else. Even he would be swallowed by the cosmos. That pure satisfaction, that joy on Javi's face, would be lost to wakefulness. Blinking into the dark, Ian feared it could never return, that it could only last in dream. In turn, the warmth in his body cooled away, a shadow fell over his heart, and he fell into the abyss.

CHAPTER ELEVEN

I an had not communicated with Hallie for seventeen days. He knew it had been seventeen days because during a bathroom break, he checked his phone and reconfirmed her last message had arrived seventeen days ago. She had sent him a picture of her smiling beside Regi and Lizzy with the message: *Feel better.*

Over those seventeen days, he had checked the message twelve times and tried to reply on five different occasions, but had stopped himself each attempt. He had nothing to say.

He had texted Lizzy three times in those seventeen days. First he had sent: *Hey, great wedding! I was just checking in on that thing about your apartment. I need to contact that Spanish woman who used to live there. Thanks!*

Then he had sent: *Hi Lizzy, just checking in. I was wondering if I could get the number to your landlord.*

And finally: *Please let me know if you can help me.*

Rohan had announced he had proposed to his fiancée in those seventeen days.

The team of three, Zoey, Rohan, and Ian, were at lunch

when Rohan had looked up with a goofy smile glued to his face.

"New news?" Zoey exclaimed.

Rohan grinned. "It took you guys long enough." He described a fantastic scene, but Ian did not listen to it much. He did pick up that it involved a dark Saturday night, a rooftop, and two people who loved each other gazing down on the lights and strangers of the City. And that Rohan had asked a woman to marry him.

"I swear, guys," he had said, "it was like something straight out of a movie."

Ian had checked papernow.com four times in those seventeen days. Their project was done, and they still had not implemented the update.

A dream had not arrived in those seventeen days. As a substitute, he received restless, empty sleep. That morning, in particular, he had woken up yearning.

Leaving the bathroom, he reached for his phone a second time and began to type a new message to Lizzy before he was stopped. Something appeared on the glass, filling his screen with a note from an unfamiliar number. It read: *Yo, it's Regi. Hope you are doing well. Can we meet up?*

After reading the text twice, he turned the phone off. He had arrived at Oscar's office.

Standing in the middle of Oscar's open doorway, split between entrance and exit, Ian waited while Oscar stood speaking on his phone. Oscar whipped his hand toward him twice, so he went in and sat down.

"Uh-huh. Yep. Okay. All right. Goodbye. I love you." Oscar tapped his phone and stood still, thinking to himself. Then he turned to look down upon Ian, casting his shadow onto the glass window behind him.

Ian could see his cogs turning, the man's mind working

toward a contrived wisdom. When he found his answer, his eyes glowed briefly, and he sat down, returning to Ian's level.

"Ian, what do you want?" he asked.

Ian had completely avoided Oscar's gaze, but this question made him focus in. "What do you mean?"

"I mean... what do you want?"

Ian found an immediate answer. "I guess I want to do a good job."

Oscar laughed. "Are you a politician? That's not a real answer."

Squirming in his chair, Ian searched for a path to end the conversation but came up short.

Oscar tapped his desk, giving time for Ian to formulate an answer, but when it became clear that nothing was coming, he continued. "I'll tell you what I wanted."

Ian held a neutral expression, but Oscar's words pulled him in.

"I wanted a family. I wanted to do good work. I wanted to be able to control my success." Oscar settled his arms on his desk and spilled his body over it, practically dripping himself before Ian. "And I'll tell you what—I got what I wanted. I got *everything*. I got a job I like, and I go home to a family I like, and I sleep well at night. But let me tell you, I worked for it. I worked damn hard. But I got what I wanted."

A well of drowning emotions pumped in Ian's chest, but he kept his face still, refusing to even give a hint of his true feelings to Oscar.

"Ian," Oscar said. Slowly, he disengaged himself from his perched position and repeated the name, stretching each syllable. "EE-uh-n," he groaned, "you know what you need? You need to figure out what you want. I want you to know what you want. And then you'll know what you need to do to get what you want. You'll have a purpose."

Oscar nodded to himself as if he'd answered his own question. "Does that make sense?"

Ian offered a faint reply. "Sure."

Each of them took a moment of silence for themselves as they both mulled over the words that had been spoken, searching for hidden truths.

"Should I go back to work?" asked Ian.

"Yes, that's fine."

As Ian stood and began to walk away, Oscar said, "Ian, one more thing."

He turned to face his boss. Oscar had put on his warm smile, like all desperation had left his body, and he was left only with a peace that told him he was right. Ian did not return the smile.

"You don't have to be so miserable."

Ian stopped mid-step and gave a robotic nod. As he left the room and walked down the halls, he stared at the gray walls. He felt something bubble in his chest, something hot and full of fury. It roiled, boiled, and bellowed, blasting steam through his head. He clutched his fists. He so desperately wanted to let the anger fly. He told himself that he knew what he wanted. He wanted Lizzy's help. He wanted to find Javi, Adriana, and Belle. He wanted them to explain their dreams. He wanted to know why they had come to him. He wanted to know what he should do with them. He wanted to know what they were telling him. He wanted peace.

"Check this out, man." Regi smiled and handed his phone over the table to Ian.

On its screen was an image: Regi with a grin, a big silly smile, splayed over a fine beach. He wore sunglasses and bathing trunks and stretched his left big toe toward some tiny dark marks in the sand near his foot. Ian squinted and zoomed in. There, next to Regi's big left foot, a tiny school of turtles waddled toward the ocean.

"I'm telling you man, they were adorable."

"Yeah, it looks nice," said Ian.

He handed the phone back, and Regi scrolled, searching for another highlight. "Look, look," he said.

Gingerly, Ian took the phone back. Replacing baby turtles was a selfie of Regi and Lizzy, grinning ear to ear, standing in front of a giant stone. As Ian handed the phone back, Regi asked, "You know how old that thing is?"

"No."

Regi concentrated at the screen and zoomed in on the monolith. He scanned it for a moment before he chuckled. "You know what? I don't know either..." He broke into hollow laughter. "I straight-up forgot! This tour guide told us. It must've been something like a thousand years old, at least. Can you believe that?"

"Wow."

"That thing lasted a *thousand* years." Regi shook his head like even he could not believe the words he was saying. "That's a long time, man. It's incredible. Something can last that long? Just crazy."

Regi took one last gaze at the image, slipped the phone into his pocket, and took a sip of his coffee. "It was a great trip, not gonna lie. South America gets it right. It's always summertime there."

Ian examined his empty half of their tiny white table and scanned the people around them. At the nearest table, a midforties man with thick rectangular glasses was reading a book. Behind them, a barista cleaned up a spill. Farther away, countless others chattered or worked in silence on laptops, all engrossed in their own universes. In the café, the men wore beards, the women wore boots, and everyone wore sweatpants.

"Regi... what do you want?"

Regi had asked him to get coffee. He had insisted that he would travel down to see him, so they had ended up at a corner café beside Ian's apartment building. Unfortunately for Ian, it had already proven to be an unbearable place. He had attempted a visit twice before but had failed to persist each time. The atmosphere simply filled him with unease. Repetitious ambient music played at a nearly imperceptible volume, but just loud enough to become an annoyance. At all times, young people and people trying to stay young crowded the space, stealing all the corners where he could have happily hidden himself away. Worst of all, the space formed a perfect rectangle, so everyone could stare at him, and he could stare at everyone. Now he stared at Regi.

"You don't want to see more pictures?" Regi asked innocently.

"Maybe later."

"Okay." Regi smiled. "By the way, did you ever hear the story about how I met Lizzy?"

Exasperated, Ian shook his head. "I heard a little of it at the wedding."

"When she walked into the office, immediately it was like…" Regi placed his index finger on his head and then clapped. "*Bam!* That's how I felt. Bam! You just know these things, right? That's how it should be. At least, I think it was like that. It becomes hard to remember."

"That's great."

"The timing was perfect. I had just become a senior associate, and here was the most beautiful paralegal I had ever laid my eyes on."

As he said his final words, Regi gave an empty stare that Ian watched with curiosity, a stare he intuitively understood. Regi was drifting somewhere else, tracing over warped memories.

"You know," Regi said slowly, "when you were talking to me at the party, I really had no idea what you were on about."

"What I was on about?"

"You're interesting. A very interesting guy, Ian. I'm not going to lie about that. Your words just struck me... They reminded me of something I had forgot."

For once, Ian looked directly at Regi, who kept his gaze away as his voice quivered and his hand trembled.

"When I spoke to you, you reminded me of this... dream I had, yeah. A while back, I had this dream where I was talking to my mom, and it was so strange. I told her that I bought Lizzy's wedding ring, but how I wasn't so sure about the whole thing. That I wasn't ready to propose to her. It was too soon; I was too uncertain. We were rushing things because of what happened. And Dad didn't really like her, he *really* didn't like her, and we'd been getting into more fights.

"But in the dream, Mama didn't say nothing. Not a word. I asked what I should do, not gonna lie, I was crying and shit. Then she smiled at me and flew into the sky and disappeared in a bright light." Regi looked at Ian with moist eyes.

"Isn't that crazy? Isn't it incredible? And that's all I needed to see. She had answered my question. I knew exactly what I had to do. The moment I woke up the next morning, I asked her to move in with me and marry me.

"And you! I don't know what sorcery you're running, or you a psychic or something, but something you said woke me up. I had forgotten my dream, forgotten it completely, and I was getting all stressed out again. But when we talked, I remembered, and I felt so much better, about everything. Lizzy doesn't give you enough credit. That's what I wanted to tell you. Thanks, man."

Ian did not know how to respond, so he said the only thing he could think of. "You're welcome."

Regi sniffled once more, before his voice returned to its

deep and jovial origins. "The thing I've pieced together now is that my dream told me what I already knew. That's all dreams can ever do. And when I saw her standing up at that altar, man, I knew. I know it's all going to work out. I know it."

"Did I also remind you about a dream at the church?"

Regi rubbed his hand against his chin. "Maybe. I only faintly remember something like that. It would've been a while ago. Maybe I forgot that one." Regi collapsed his arms down and swung his hefty body back up into his chair. "That was pretty intense."

"Yeah," said Ian with a strained voice. "By the way, did Lizzy ever get the messages I sent her?"

"Oh, yes!" Regi sprang up. "That was the main thing I came to tell you—you've got to stop harassing Lizzy."

Ian froze. *Harassing?* "I'm not harassing Lizzy," he sputtered. "I only texted her three times, maybe only a couple more."

"Yeah. I know, I know. It's just, she's going through a lot, so much is changing. She needs some space. And you were messaging her during the entire honeymoon." Regi chuckled.

There it was again. That anger that had smoldered after work reignited in a brief, concentrated bang. These people didn't get it. Ian smashed his fist on the table. "Well, I need her help!"

Regi backed up, and some coffee spilled over, sending tiny droplets onto the floor. He said nothing for a second and instead studied Ian with confused eyes. Then he waved his hands up and down toward Ian, as if trying to cool off a fire. "Simmer down, simmer down, young man." He laughed it off. "I gotcha. It's just that her hormones are all out of whack."

"What do you mean?"

Regi nodded. "She's gotten real crazy right now. It's like month eight, after all."

"What?"

Regi's face transformed from laid-back to surprised as reality dawned on him. "She didn't tell you?"

Ian shook his head.

"Ah, I see. She's told a lot of people. I guess I haven't kept good track. You see… Lizzy's pregnant. Really pregnant."

Ian stared at Regi. His smile indicated excitement, his inflection rang bubbly, but his eyes screamed panic. Ian placed his elbow on the table and leaned his head against a loose fist. He stayed like that, thinking in silence, before he said, "I see."

Then he peeked over to his right, and Regi followed his lead. The setting around them had shifted. The man next to them with the book now leaned on the edge of his seat, after aligning his ear directly in parallel to his interesting neighbors. A teenager behind them had paused the show on her computer. Regi and Ian waited for a moment, until it seemed the two strangers had grown tired of listening and resumed their lives.

After the pause, Regi asked, "So what help did you need?"

Ian chose his words carefully, methodically plucking them out one by one from his mind. He wanted to lay them in front of Regi as simply as possible. There were things Regi didn't need to understand. "There was a woman Lizzy met when she moved into the city, into her first apartment. I need to find that woman. I've called the building's office four times, but they haven't responded. I need Lizzy to help me get in touch with her old landlord."

"Ah, I see," Regi said. "Why do you need to find her?"

Ian glanced at Regi's golden ring on his left hand and listened to the terribly irritating music looping for the third time, just above his left ear. It was all becoming too much. Already he wanted to go back to sleep, and it had barely passed ten a.m. He sighed. "I just do."

Regi sized up Ian. "Well, all right, then. I have a plan for you. A brilliant plan. A brilliantly simple plan."

"What plan?"

Regi bumped the top of the table. "Why don't you just go to the place?"

"What do you mean?"

"I mean, just go to the dang apartment building and find the landlord." Regi crossed his arms, squeezing his massive forearms. "You don't need to wait for him to answer the phone. Just go and get an answer!" He grinned. "You feel me?"

In truth, Regi had given Ian exactly the answer he needed and feared. By then, he had already known what he needed to do, the truth in his heart, the truth that Regi had so easily reached. He needed to go, even if he had been passively avoiding it. Instead of wallowing and wondering, he would have to walk. Regi was right. It was time.

"I feel you," said Ian.

"Okay, then."

The two made small talk, nodded, and prepared to leave. On the way out, Regi said, "By the way, your girlfriend is a real one. She's cool."

"Who?"

"I think her name was Kallie, or Raleigh, maybe? That girl you brought to the wedding. She showed me and Lizzy pictures of these great sculptures she made. They were wild."

"We don't have a relationship."

"Ah, I see. Well, maybe you should work on that."

ON THE SUBWAY to Lizzy's old apartment, Ian fumbled with his phone. He had hunched over, keeping his head in his lap, hidden from his fellow passengers. There, he opened up a map of the world and zoomed in and out, aimlessly jumping from nation to nation. He journeyed from east to west and to everything in between. He stopped by a village in Mongolia, scrolled to a city in Africa. He dragged across oceans and pinched to the South, where he stopped in curiosity and soaked in entire histories, drawn by blood and anguish and victory, with just a glance of some lines. And for his finale, he returned north, to the City, where he located himself and the train on the map.

He had explored the entire world all in the time it took to travel 5.7 miles. Only when the cold voice of the robot conductor called out his stop did he lift his head and notice they had emerged out of the underground and a new neighborhood had been birthed underneath them, full of tired life and drab colors.

He trotted down the stairs and kicked old snow off his boots. All the pure white powder that had once painted the City had turned into a melting, dirty slush. Almost slipping down a step, he realized had been in the City for months. The darkest days had passed, and now the sun survived a little longer before it faded into night. New Year's had arrived stealthily, with slow days dissolving quickly into a new year. He could hardly recall the event; he had stayed in the City during the holidays, sleeping, eating, working, whittling time away. He had told his mother it would be wise for him to save travel money for another day.

He arrived and stood in front of Lizzy's old apartment building, then walked up the building's steps and pushed on the gate. It would not move, so he rattled it, trying to break the lock down, but still it would not budge. From behind his shoulder, the cold wind slapped him and bit into his neck. In a sudden desperation, he threw his whole body into the effort and pressed his legs into the hard ground as he shoved his back, arms, and mind into the gate.

Every point of contact was painful. The iron metal seared frost into his bare hands, made his knuckles numb and red, and kept his spine frozen. But he persisted. He pulled and pushed and pulled, yet made no progress. Eventually it started to vibrate, shaking along with the concrete, as both the metal and

Ian trembled in fear of an incoming train. Only once Ian's body began to shudder uncontrollably did he finally rip himself off the icy bars and stumble over his feet.

Falling down, he screamed unintelligibly into the bitter air and scraped both of his hands on the ground. He rolled over and pressed himself against the slope of the stoop. There, on the ground, he compressed himself into a ball, wrapped his coat tightly around himself, and gazed out into the City.

Like ants, the pedestrians crawled through the block, between its shops, apartments, and the train, each one trying to ignore the cold and the man on the ground but glancing all the same. They were no better than the roaches that occasionally scattered across his sink at night, all racing right in front of him while he lay curled up, trying to ignore them.

"What the hell am I doing?" he muttered to the cold.

He waited, searching out into the gray of the City with helpless eyes, until his question met an answer.

A woman, bent over and resigned to carrying time's weight, limped down the street toward the stoop. Her every step was an ordeal, with constant trembling, tottering, and bending, as if she would break at any second. When she reached the stoop's steps, she stopped entirely to survey their topography, for they marked her Everest.

After making a final decision, she pressed all her strength into her knees and took the initial heroic leap up.

And made it.

She landed with a soft thud and stood proud. Then again she leapt, and again. After each successful attempt, she stopped and recuperated for the next challenge. Occasionally during her arduous journey, she looked up at Ian with some aggressive longing.

He watched her with mild curiosity, then impatience, then acceptance. "Do you need some help?" he asked.

The woman gave him a small smile and nodded twice in

rapid succession. He grunted and peeled himself off the concrete and rose. He took her arm and helped her climb up each remaining step to the gate. In his hands, he could feel how tiny she was, how shrunken.

"Thank you! Thank you!" she cried and shook his hand. Slowly, she pulled out her key.

"No problem."

While she took her time to open up the entrance, she asked, "What name?"

"My name?"

She nodded.

"Ian."

"Hi Ian. I Lee Jeong-sook. From Korea. Long story."

"Ah, okay, Lee. I'm looking for the landlord."

She pushed open the door and looked at him, startled. "What do you want with him? He no good."

"I have business with him."

"Oh. Me too." She laughed. "He ask for rent. I move here month ago. Still no pay yet. But don't worry!" She laughed like she was sharing the greatest secret in the world. "We have money, we will pay, just not want to pay *him*. He no good, very mean man."

"That's great," Ian said slowly. "Do you know where he lives?"

"Yes. He above. Right above."

"Great. Where do you live?"

"3E."

The two walked in, and Lee turned to Ian. "Thank you, young man," she said, but he did not hear her; he had already opted for the stairs. She stared up at him as he dashed up each step while she waited for the elevator.

IAN HEAVED when he arrived at the fourth floor. His stomach

bellowed and burned, busting under the pressure; the climb had done him in. After only a few months, his body had slowed, weakened, and swelled from long days of sitting and staring at a screen. He exhaled twice, lifted his feet, and waddled toward the gray door.

In front of him, black letters read: #4E.

He stopped, scratching his head, wondering what he would say. Then he shook his head. It didn't matter. Some things just need to get done, and this was just one of them. He rang the old gray doorbell.

And waited.

For thirty seconds more, he waited.

And he waited some more.

Then he rang again, twice, and instantly the door ripped open.

"Whatchya want?" Standing in front of Ian was a pasty smushed rectangle of a man. Wide and short, he was equipped with four rings on his left hand and a bald square-shaped head that shined like yellow chrome under the fluorescent lighting.

"I says whatchya want? Yer plumbing broke?"

"No… I don't live here."

The rectangle closed its eyes and vigorously shook its head. "What? Whatchya want, then? Am I not allowed to enjoy my weekend?"

"Of course," said Ian, "but I have a question."

"That's what I fuckin' asked you! Whatchya want?"

The rectangle began to tap its sides, ready to close the door.

Ian met the rectangle's pace and slurred his words, rushing them out. "I called you. I called you a week ago."

"I don't remember this. I don't get many calls."

"I called you about an Adriana. A Hispanic lady."

The rectangle inspected Ian, staring him down, and

became a man again as he slowed his words. "That's right. Yeah... I do remember. You called me last week."

He leaned against his door and stretched his legs across the entrance, blocking the inside from the out. "You shouldn't call that much," he mumbled. "Ye'd think one would get the message."

Ian leaned in. "So you do know her?"

The man looked Ian up and down and said, "What do you want with those *spics*?" He casually explained, "I usually don't look for spics for tenants. Them Chinese are better with the rent. I only let those two stay because the money was good. They had that one friend, that blonde babe, whose money was good."

Ian blinked twice. "What do you mean?"

"What do you mean? Oh, what do you mean?" The man mocked. "Like I said, whatchya want with *them*? I don't have to say *shit* about nothing. They not here anymore, that's it. That's all I got for you. They gone now."

Ian saw the man was rapidly hardening back into a rectangle, with his brain bending into one thick prism. "Look... I just need to find them. I just need to talk to them."

The door began to close. "Well, I can't help you with that. That old lady got gone, like, two years ago. Honest to god, I knows how I sound, but I liked her. She was a nice one, till she got all strange."

"Wait, wait." Ian grabbed the door, holding it open. "Do you have her number? Adriana's number, or Javi's?"

The rectangle clenched its jaw. "I'm fairly certain that guy's number won't do you no good. The woman's, maybe. Maybe. I'd haveta dig that up." It looked back to Ian and performed some basic arithmetic. "Like I says before. What's your interest? I'm just a humble property owner and business proprietor. I ain't looking for trouble."

"She's a… friend." Ian nodded. "I just want to talk to her, honestly."

The rectangle offered the tiniest hint of a smile and broke its shape for a final time. The math was easy. "Okay, then," the man said. "Gimme a hundred bucks, and I'll look for her number."

Ian rifled with his pockets, but he knew he had nothing to find. "Sorry, I don't carry cash. I can send you money over the phone."

The man waved his hand in front of his nose. He made a face like Ian's words were hot garbage, straight from a world he did not care to understand or enjoy. "Money over the *phone?* I don't deal with that shit. Cash is king, baby." He opened his eyes wide and rubbed his fingers. "Ye understand? Money, *mon-ay?*"

Ian inspected at the man up and down. This short, pale, squished glob of a man. This was where his dreams had led him. Resigned, he pleaded, "Look, I'll give you my wallet, *if* you help me. It's leather. It was a gift; it's real nice."

"Lemme see it."

Ian pulled out his wallet and slowly placed it in the man's outstretched hand. The man stroked its leather and inspected its wear. Then he daintily pulled out all of the IDs and cards, dropping some into Ian's hands and others onto the floor. After his show, he said, "You're right. This is nice. I like this a lot."

"That's great. Can you give me her number?"

"Aight, gimme a fuckin' minute." Then the door snapped to a close, and the wallet disappeared with it. In under a minute, another shard of another memory of another time had dissolved.

Two minutes later, Ian knocked. "Hello? Hello?"

"Gimme a fucking minute!"

Ian gave him a minute, and the man wiggled back out of his door and handed Ian a wrinkled piece of paper.

"Here," he said. "That was her cellie when she lived here. Hope you find whatchya looking for. Bye." Then he slammed the door and said no more.

Ian gazed at the number, then pulled out his phone and rushed to tap it in. He hadn't been prepared to come this far, to be so close. His heart crashed in its cavity and sent blood gushing into his belly. The dreams of so many flashed, diving up and down the waves of his mind. He laughed, he cackled, his glee echoed across the tiny hallway. This was it. Soon he would be able to sleep easy again.

He lifted his phone to his ear and heard:

Ring!

Ring!

Ring!

Ring!

Ring…

Ring…

"Please leave a message after the beep."

BEEP!

Ian whispered into the phone, "Hi. Hello. Please call back this number as soon as possible, please. Thanks." He gave his number and hung up.

He banged his fist against the door and shouted, "Are you sure that's the right number?" The rectangle didn't respond, so Ian picked up his cards and IDs from the floor, looked to the end of the hallway and walked down the stairs, heading home.

B elle faced the man across from her, tapped on the table twice, and asked, "Do you like the food?"

He was slumped back with gray hair spilling out of his button-down shirt. He poked at his half-eaten filet mignon, sighed, and let a tired frown speak for him.

In front of her lay an untouched loaf of bread, and her eyes were hidden behind black plastic sunglasses.

Together, united by their silence, they roasted slowly outside on the patio as summer sun seeped into their skin. Around them, other patrons chattered indiscriminately in foreign tongues, offering no easy alternative conversation to listen and latch on to. But at last, breaking the table's stillness, the man set his fork across his plate and crossed his arms.

"So?" she asked.

"It's okay," he muttered. He looked toward Ian's direction. His face screamed frustration and failing patience, so Ian avoided his stare by examining their surroundings.

It seemed they were no longer in the City, as the environment appeared manageable. Small brick buildings and humble cobblestones lined the streets, and the natives, spread across the patio, were dressed in a calculated mix of casual sophistication —they still wore pants in the heat. Born by way of an old world, they spoke, moved, and ate slower. They sipped on life while the savages of the City slurped it. Even the wind seemed to move at a snail's pace. And from above hung the restaurant's low sign, whose shadow covered Belle and the man. It read: *Boulangerie Du Palais.*

Click.

Ian turned around and saw what the man had been staring at. A crowd had crept up the street. Each member held blocky cameras with silver finishes and hurriedly snapped pictures of whatever captured their attention, until something else stole their focus.

The man checked his watch, a piece of pure gold and glittering diamonds. "Time runs so fast," he said. "How about you? Do you like it? Are you done yet?"

Belle picked up her bread and took one small quick bite. She nodded. "It's good. I'm not quite finished."

The man draped his arm onto the side of the table. "What about that man? The Spanish man?"

"What about him?"

He resumed staring at the crowd and said nothing.

Ian inched toward the table and studied Belle. Once again, she had cleaned and polished herself, appearing pristine, without a speck of grime or a mislaid strand of hair.

Her new look, her new poise, puzzled Ian. From dream to dream, dreamer to dreamer, her image had drifted from that of a ghoul by the river to melting light. Even in her own dreams, she went from practically a princess in a dress to a crisis on train tracks. Her self-image appeared to be reliably unreliable.

Again she nibbled on the bread and said quietly, "It's not

permanent. It's not. Nothing's ever permanent. He just needed some help."

The man grabbed a loaf of bread of his own and gobbled it down. Between bites, he asked, "What help? What are you really helping?"

Belle smiled weakly. "Without me, he'd still be riding his bike twenty miles a day."

As she spoke, her hand trembled, and her sunglasses dipped down her nose. She picked up her bread and took another slow, careful bite into its brown flesh. Then she flinched. Her face twitched and her glasses tumbled off her nose, shattering on the stone pavement. She covered her face with her hands, closed her eyes, and pulled her head back.

Ian inched up. He could see something on the bread glaring from the sun.

She slowly pulled her neck back and looked at the man with terror.

Ian came up further still. For sure there was something. Something had lodged itself into the bread's hard crust, like a piece of corn sticking out.

Belle whined and her eyes watered.

Ian crouched and took a look.

No.

He stumbled back, gagged, and spat on the ground. His face twisted, growing red, flushed with disgust.

That can't be right.

He took another reluctant peek to verify what he found, even though he knew that he didn't need to check. What he had seen was impossible to miss.

Sticking out on the side of the bread was a yellowed tooth.

The man glared at her. "Honey, I already paid for the meal. It was a fixed menu."

"Okay, Dad."

Tenderly, Belle picked up the piece of bread again and this

time took a wide bite. Then came the crunch. A sudden, trapped shock gripped her face. All her teeth emptied out of her mouth. For a moment, they desperately hung on to the bread, refusing to yield to gravity, but then they failed and released their hold. They fell, shining like yellow diamonds under the bright sun.

When they landed, they clattered across the table, landing on plates, in cups, and in all the crevices in between. Dad swept his arm to scoop up the teeth that had landed in front of him and began to pick out a couple from his plate.

"You shouldn't lose teeth," he muttered as he picked up each one and slid them into his right pocket.

Belle tried to speak with her mouth closed, but all she could muster was a weak blur of sounds and saliva. Nothing comprehensible.

"How much did we pay for your dentist? Now you'll need to go back."

She opened her mouth and reached inside. Nothing was there except empty gums and a scared tongue.

"That man is taking too much of your time," Dad said nonchalantly. "Have you found a new job yet?" As he spoke, Ian could hear the sound of the train picking up in the distance and felt a small tremor emerge.

She pushed her chair back and stood up, still tracing her fingers over her empty gums. Simultaneously, the crowd on the street surrounded the restaurant and began to spin their cameras around.

"Ey-needa guh."

She sped toward the end of the patio, while her father waved to the crowd and laughed. "Honey, look. The crowd loves it."

Ian stepped back, dodging the tourists as they engulfed the restaurant, and then found himself befuddled. At the front of the pack, leading the charge, was Adriana. She seemed unusually alive and well as she swung her arms violently at Belle and shouted, *"BRUJA! Eres bruja!"*

In the small gaps between Adriana and the rest of the crowd, he could see flashes of Belle, who was being pushed back by them. It seemed she would be trapped, swallowed up by the tourists who scrunched her in, but after one final desperate struggle, she found an opening. She managed to rip open a hole in the swarm, jump through it, and break out into a full sprint.

At first Ian hesitated as he stared at Adriana, but when he smelled fresh sweat and sensed the blistering air, he experienced a sudden tight squeeze in his chest. He knew it wasn't his fear, that he shouldn't listen, that it was just dream, but lately every nocturnal sensation had become too powerful to resist. He opened his body to Belle's instincts and received one clear message: Go.

He ran after her.

She sprinted down the wide street, then took a sudden turn right down a narrow alley. She ignored the colorful buildings to her left and right. She ignored the old-world homes built by forgotten men. She ignored their stories, their spiraling pasts. She just kept running. She needed to leave, and with every step, the sound of the train's scream grew louder and louder until its shaking reached an apex.

She turned another corner and waited in front of a dead end. Ian stepped closer to her, examining how she trembled, how nervous she was, how her skin had begun to gray once more.

He awaited wakefulness, but it did not come. Instead, the train's scream slowed and the ground calmed, until both ceased entirely.

At the dead end, she stared at the ancient bricks of the old city. Confused, he walked up and stroked the mortar. It was a dull sensation but a sensation nonetheless: the hardened paste felt cold.

Then before their eyes, the earthy clay transformed into glass and steel, revealing the dark metal of a subway car door. Once finished, the door opened. Belle walked in, and Ian followed.

Inside the car, their bodies took on darker, uglier hues, with the sun's colors drowned out and replaced by fluorescent yellow. And once the train started moving, the somber space only dulled further. As they rolled forward, the windows left behind quaint structures and tiny corridors, replacing them with the pitch dark of the underground.

The car was empty except for Belle and Ian. She sat down and looked out the black window. Alone, she whimpered, "Heulow?"

Ian sat beside her and wanted to console her, ask what made her so afraid, but he did nothing, for he knew she would not be able to hear his voice nor feel his touch.

Then, at the end of the car, a door slid open. Standing beyond its threshold was Javi. He strutted in, looking oddly tall and oddly strong, while he wore his construction uniform and a concerned face.

"Heup me."

He said nothing. He simply walked up to her and embraced her and held her in his steady arms.

Belle quickly stopped crying. The train's sound picked up again, and the ground regained a mild roll. As the two cradled each other, her face recovered its original form. Her teeth reemerged, and her tears dried. She reached into her pocket and pulled out a clump of white powder, but Javi took her hand. "Not now. Maybe later."

Ian watched the two of them as the train around them dissolved into darkness and its sound diminished, disappearing into the distance. He remembered the peace he had achieved watching the two of them above the earth, the serenity, the inspiration. Unfortunately, that was not what he saw in the dim of the car. Looking at the two of them under the train's yellow bulb, he only felt anxious. Belle's muscles were tight, and the gleam in her eyes was weak.

Javi embraced Belle while she clutched him.

CHAPTER TWELVE

The screen had a dead pixel near its bottom-right corner. 2,073,599 tiny flawless squares of light composed the functional portion of the monitor, and each one could display a single bountiful color of infinite hues and harmonies, but only by working together could they craft a cascade of images. They shifted constantly, sending pictures floating and prancing around, all designed to splash delight over any user. All except for the dead pixel, for it could only render black.

Two minutes earlier, Ian had spotted the minuscule black square and stopped working. When he did so, the monitor's stream of change froze, while the other pixels waited for his command. But he only stared at the screen, at one spot in particular, and hesitated to interact with its magic. He did not move the mouse, nor did he touch the keyboard. One single dead pixel had shattered a perfect digital illusion.

And the dead pixel, trapped flat in its home, a two-dimensional prison, could do nothing about its predicament. It could not turn to its neighbors for aid, nor could they turn to it and notice how it did not shine. Instead, it only had one option: stare forward. It stared back at Ian, and he stared at it, and though neither would like to admit it, they both understood the other perfectly.

Then his phone rang and broke the distraction.

He clumsily pulled it out of his pocket and swung it in front of his tired eyes. The caller ID read: *Unknown.*

He ignored it and muted the device. In recent months, too many robotic salespeople had demanded too much of him. They wanted his time, his insurance, his social security number, his life. No longer would he even amuse them.

After a quick wake-up shake of his head, he stood up, took a five-minute trudge to the water fountain, and headed down for lunch.

It was only 11:27 a.m., so the cafeteria was mostly empty, as was planned. Over the last few weeks, Ian had developed an intuition: He knew if he showed by 11:27, and no later, he would always get the spot, *his spot*, a tight corner table in the back half of the cafeteria, beside a clear window and beautifully isolated from the crowd.

He waited in line, chose his sandwich, and plopped down in his seat. After a long breath, he slowly began to munch. He licked his teeth after some bites to ensure they were still fastened tight; the image of Belle's yellowed tooth stuck in her bread had lingered.

In passing days, he had begun to see the shadows of others on strangers' faces. Earlier that week on the train, he had pushed his way up to an old woman who was crouched by the door. She looked to have the right hair and the right height, but when he reached her, he realized she had only been a delusion, a stranger, not Adriana. She smiled at him anyway, nodded, and then went away. The same had happened for faint lookalikes of Javi and Belle. All illusions. None were those whom he needed to find.

He sighed and pulled out his phone. The small screen

could melt worries away, replace them with diversions. He flicked twice, tapped once, and pondered an old message.

Hallie had written him some days ago: *Hallo! What's up? You good?*

He gave it more than a glance and then took off. He twirled through comfortable cyberspace and refilled his cup of vicarious experience within a river of pixelated faces. Occasionally he, half searching and half hiding, would catch a glimmer of Hallie within digital lakes before he scurried away. Yet everywhere he went, he somehow managed to stumble his way back to her. Her image had been weaved into his web.

It seemed both on the train and on the screen, everyone everywhere looked at everything and could find anything in everything. On the train, strangers stared at him, and he stared back at them, and they each planted an idea of the other in their own heads. On the screen, faces distorted themselves, posing and pushing for the best image, pretending they had control over their story.

None of it was truly real, Ian knew, more like their truth's best angle, the bright side of a mostly dark moon. He knew people's truth only fully came out at night, when they were asleep. He had seen it.

Still, both the train and the digital world offered an alluring power: escapism through others. And the screen proved to have a crucial advantage over the train. On the screen, the stranger could not stare back.

After his cup began to overrun, he pivoted to his voicemail box, which held one unread message. In his experience, the voicemail box served as a rarely useful tool, filled with messages that carried no weight, but at least it offered another distraction. He held the phone against his ear and pressed play.

"Hello, this is Elana. I am calling back from Albin Elder Care Institute. We received a call on one of our patient's phone. To contact us, please visit our website at albininstitute.com or call us back at…"

Ian shivered. His heart skipped a beat.

Today will be the day.

Out of an unadulterated excitement, he banged the table with a hard fist, ended the call, and quickly searched for the facility.

He was only an hour and twelve minutes away. Only two trains and a bus separated him from her.

After stuffing the remainder of his sandwich down his throat, he rose and hustled out of the cafeteria. Before he made it out, a soft voice addressed him. He skidded to a stop and turned. Zoey and Rohan were entering.

Smiling, Zoey waved. "Hey, Ian, want to grab a bite?"

He offered a weak gesture in return and whispered, "No, actually, I already ate." He kept marching forward.

Behind him, he heard, "Ah, okay. See you later."

He walked out the door, then accelerated to a jog. He glided through melting slush and sliced through vicious winds. They would not stop him, nothing would. All he needed was her and her story.

His efforts brought him to the underground. There he waited five minutes and found his first train swerving into the station. Far from prime time, the car contained only three others: a homeless man slumped in the back, a middle-aged woman with old skin, and a teenager who leaned against the door. He ignored them all. They were wandering strangers. They did not matter. He knew himself to be on a vital path. After sliding into the nearest available seat, he cradled his head in his lap.

Finally, he had a chance to think.

What will I say to her? What will she tell me? Will she understand?

Questions rolled around in his head like marbles without friction. They would not stop; they did not have an end in sight, nor did he want them to stop.

Why does she fear Belle? Why did she see Papa's face so strangely? Why did she shake and shiver?

They invigorated him and sent concentrated dashes of hope, fear, curiosity, and amazement straight into his bloodstream, masking his fears, his holes.

When did she take over the apartment from Javi and Belle? Where can I find them? Did she see María again?

In the time that followed, it felt like the train could not go any slower, but eventually even seconds turned into minutes, which turned into stops, which turned into a final bus ride.

His phone had brought him far away from the City's heart, past Lizzy's old apartment, into the outer rim of the metropolis. During the commute, the electric pulse that kickstarted the journey had been partially stowed away, but there was no denying it now. He tapped his foot against the steel of the bus in a futile attempt to dissipate his excitement. He could not stop the churn of energy, not while the bus's windows instructed him how to feel.

There it is.

He could see it across the street, a modest white building, flat and wide. Its front entrance was no glass wonder; it had simple painted doors. A line of windows and small grass lawns wrapped around its walls, each painted by melting snow, and embedded above its awning, strong metal letters read: *Albin Elder Care Institute.*

Finally the bus rolled to a stop, and Ian got off in a daze. He floated across the street with light steps and stopped himself in front of the entrance. He peeked into a window, pushed himself forward, and entered.

The lobby had a yellow hue like the trains he had grown accustomed to, but that did not diminish his buzz. Nor did the empty chairs or the lone turned-off TV. In fact, the entire space was empty except for the reception counter, where two women sat looking bored. He took a deep breath and walked up to the nearest one.

"Hi. I got a call."

She peered at him. "You need to check in, honey. Right here." She pointed at a clipboard on top of the counter. "Who called you?"

He wrote down his contact information. "I called. I got a call back from Alana. She told me to come here."

The other woman raised her head from her computer. "My name is Elana."

"Yes, that was it. I'm sorry, Elana."

The woman in front of Ian turned to Elana. "Who's he here to visit?"

"That's a good question." Elana rolled her chair over next to her coworker. "We collect our patient's phones for... ease of management. The phone you called wasn't labeled. Just a really old flip phone. Who are you trying to see?"

Ian stumbled on his words. "Adria... Adriana!"

The two women looked at each other. Elana asked, "Do we have an Adriana?"

The other shook her head. "No. I don't think we do."

He leaned over the counter. "Adriana is here. She must be. I know she is."

"Please stand behind the counter, sir," Elana said.

He slunk back, barely floating behind her invisible line.

The other woman typed on her computer and read the screen to herself. "You're right... We do have an Adriana. You must've been talking about Adri."

Elana looked hard at Ian. "What's your relation?"

He paused. "I'm a friend... I'm very close to her brother."

Elana stood up and walked around the counter. "Well, you're the second visitor Adri has received, I think. It's been a while. I'm fairly certain the last time someone was here was the day she moved in! I hope she'll be glad to see you."

Ian could not believe it. He was only a walk away from reconnecting the shattered visions that had become his every night. He was so close to her. Every step felt like a step toward absolution. He would fulfill his purpose, connect past to present, and finally understand: why him, why he carried their dreams, what they were trying to tell him.

Elana pushed open the door and revealed a hallway with clean white walls. Along the walls were a series of doors, and in the middle of it, an elderly man moved slowly, pushing himself along with a plastic walker.

Elana waved and said loudly, "Hi, Maurice."

He turned, surprised, and waved at Ian with an open smile. Half his teeth were missing.

She lowered her breath. "They don't get a lot of visitors here, so you're a breath of fresh air."

Ian tiptoed around Maurice, who remained stuck in the center of the hallway, being too slow to get out of their way. They journeyed deeper around the edge of the building, strutting in silence, but Ian heard no quiet; his heart was too loud. It pumped throughout his whole body, every contraction sending shockwaves across his nervous system.

Elana turned a final corner. "We're here."

He could not contain it any longer. Everything wanted to burst. He felt trapped in the millisecond while everything else moved at light speed.

Elana grasped the knob. "Be slow with her. She's not in great shape."

As the door opened, Ian's first sight was a wide window that revealed a bleak world of highways and cars zipping past each other. Then as it swung further, he spotted the edge of a white bed on top of a black bed frame, until finally, it opened entirely. And there she was. Adriana.

She was lying in bed with her eyes wide open, staring straight into space. Her skin had grown impossibly shriveled, and her eyes even more ancient, far older than when he had first met her by the roundabout, but there was no denying it. She was Adriana.

When they walked in, she did not turn to face them.

"Adri, how are you doing? You have a guest."

Her mouth hung open, and she twisted her head up and down. It seemed she looked everywhere except their direction, as if she were searching for something she couldn't find.

Ian puffed up his chest and approached her with careful steps. "Adriana? I need to talk to you."

She did not respond; she only mumbled in unintelligible Spanish.

"I've been searching for you, Adriana. I've been seeing so much, so I needed to see you. I needed to meet you... Adriana?"

Still she did not look at him. Instead she squirmed her body around, twisting her form, searching for an unreachable comfort. Under the hospital lights, her once rich brown skin had grown the palest he had ever seen.

Something was not right.

Ian opened his mouth, but his lips quivered. He could not find the courage to speak.

Elana spoke for him. "I'm sorry," she said plainly, "but she's at the point where she doesn't understand anything. It's been like this for a couple months now."

Ian spun back around to Elana. Terror had taken over his face, freezing his features and trapping his spirit in a confused fear. Elana was completely nonchalant.

Slowly, he turned back to Adriana. "Adriana, I need to talk to you."

Once again, she did not respond.

"Like I said, she's not going to understand you. She barely

remembered any English when she arrived, and she was already forgetting her Spanish too. Now it's all gone."

Ian could feel his eyes growing wet. He snapped at Elana, "I'll decide that."

He went up close to her, close enough to hear her weak breaths and her strained body. This was the woman whose dreams were so vivid, the woman who made earthquakes, who faced her father, who rode the river.

"Adriana," he said softly, "I saw everything. I saw you. I saw your terrible dreams, and your good ones. I saw your panic, I saw your father, and I saw the river. I want to hear it from you, and I want to tell you what I've seen too. It's a cold city to be alone in. We can talk about it all. Take your time, it's all right. I just have a few questions."

He waited for her, and when she didn't say anything, he continued. "I want you to know that I met Javi. He's fantastic; his dreams are fantastic. You couldn't imagine. He sees fountains of light, he sees the Earth from the Moon, he sees above everything. I can tell why you care about him so much. His smile can light up anything. He's wonderful."

Tears began to well and flow freely. "And Adi, I saw you. I saw you young. I saw you on the river with María. Do you remember that? It was such a special night."

Adriana shook her head and contorted her body. For a moment, her eyes met his, and he smiled. *She does understand me,* he thought.

But a moment only lasts a moment. She twitched again, and when her head turned away, she revealed the diaper hidden under her blanket.

Ian pulled his hands up and glared at them. They were shaking uncontrollably.

Behind him, he heard, "She spits out her food now, so we have started to give her crushed painkillers in yogurt."

He slowly turned around. Elana was leaning against the door, casually watching the two of them.

"How can you talk like that?"

She gave him a counterfeit concerned look. "I'm sorry. We just get used to it."

He grabbed the side of his head. *Adriana.* He didn't even want to look at her, but he had no choice.

He turned again and whispered, "Adriana…"

Even in his fogged vision, the truth in front of him was plain enough for him to see, for anyone to see. The old woman of their dreams had deteriorated. She had turned into a pile of blood and bones and mumbles. Agony stretched across her face. She did not know where she was, nor who she was. Her existence was pain, and that was who she had become: pain.

She was no longer human.

Ian stumbled back and landed on the floor. Something had finally snapped. He could feel it. His body knew something was deeply wrong. His mind knew it too, but he would need time to figure out what had happened. Something did not feel right. Nothing about this was right.

Elana tapped him on the shoulder. "You all right?"

He shook his head with shocked eyes. Then he pushed himself off the floor. "Yes."

He walked up close to Elana. "Who was Adriana's other visitor?"

She stepped back. "Let's talk about this in the reception area."

He stepped forward. "Why can't you tell me now?"

Elana twisted her mouth. "It's confidential, and we need to talk about Adriana's bill."

He nearly jumped up and down, but he forced himself to breathe. "Who's paying for her stay? Who visited her when she moved in? Please, tell me."

"Let's go to the computer and talk about this."

Reluctantly, Ian listened. Elana walked out of the room and motioned for him to leave. He turned to face Adriana one more time, watched her mumble and stare into an abyss. He watched her twitch and roll. He waited for her to look at him, to give him any kind of indication she was there, that any piece of her was there. But eventually it became all too clear, and he could not lie to himself any longer. There was nothing.

He closed his eyes then left.

WITH EVERY STEP toward the lobby, his legs grew weaker. They felt heavy and clumsy and dumb. By the time he arrived, he was barely able to stand. He leaned against the counter to support himself.

Elana tapped into the computer. "Our records say that Adri has a $35,700 outstanding bill. Are you ready to pay for her stay?"

"What?"

"The woman who was paying for her stay previously has not sent a check for a few months, and Adri does not have any insurance or even any documentation to apply for national health insurance. If we can't get that, we may need to remove her from the facility."

"What are you talking about?"

"Our care is high quality, but it does come at a cost. Like I said, can you close Adriana's bill?"

Ian grabbed his eyebrows and pushed his skin together. He could barely think; it seemed every word came two seconds after the next. "Who was paying for her stay before?"

"That's confidential."

Venom spawned in his blood and seeped into his tongue. No more of this. "Listen. You tell me who she was. Give me her number. Give me her name. And I'll get her to pay you the damn bill."

Elana froze, stopped talking, and reexamined Ian as if she had just met him for the first time. Then she nodded.

"Let's see… I found Adriana's initial move-in record."

"*Who is it?*"

"Her name is Belle Miller."

Elana gave him Belle's number and said a quick goodbye. He said nothing. He ambled out of the facility, and once out of view, he collapsed onto the wet snowy grass. He crawled forward and pressed himself against the facility's cold wall, hiding from their windows.

The shake in his hands had not ceased, and with trembling fingers, he worked to pull out his phone and punch in the number. Finally, after his fourth attempt, he entered it in correctly.

He wrote: *Hi Belle. I'm a friend of Javi and Adriana. I was wondering if there was a time I could meet up with you, and Javi too. If he's free. Thanks.*

Send.

After he sent the message, he let his whole body go. He let his face fall flat into slushy ground and remain there. His head hurt, his eyes stung, and his hands burned from the cold. After five minutes, he felt his phone vibrate. He weakly reached for it and read the caller ID: *Oscar.* He let it go to voicemail.

On the ground, he stared into the dark. He did not move, for he couldn't move. He could stay there forever and let his body sink into the earth. The earth would swallow him, his weight, his failure. The earth would hide everything.

But soon the wind returned, cut into his back, and forced him to leave.

★★★★★

The old boy and the old man sat together. They were outside their old home, enjoying a warm breeze passing by.

Ian hesitantly approached them, slowly easing up; the summer's sweet smell could not be denied.

He stood next to the two of them, father and son, who sat in rickety chairs painted blue. Together the three of them relaxed on a hill as they watched a slow world tick away, feather grass swaying and a river flowing.

The old man turned to his thirty-year-old son. "You want to cross the river, huh?"

Javi turned to his father and shook his head. "No, Papá, have I not told you? I've already left. I've gone much farther."

Papá again, Ian thought. He could still remember the monster who'd invaded Adriana's dream, the man without a face, but looking at him now, perhaps he was never a monster. After all, Ian considered, the worst memories were the ones that stuck around the longest. Perhaps that was all Adriana could hold on to now, even in dream.

Atop the hill, under a friendly sun, Papá's voice carried a softness, a compassion, a natural love that poured out like honey, covering Javi in tenderness. "Oh, I see," he said, then laughed. "That's who you've always been, who you're meant to be—a stone that will ripple the whole world." He kept his gaze fixated on the water. "But I'm not sure if your sister will follow you. She's always been a little different."

"She's already north. She was afraid, but I convinced her. I told her to come, so she came. I'm helping her."

"Oh, I see." Papá kicked the dirt and breathed in the air. "What about the woman? The woman you're seeing?"

"What about her?" Javi asked.

The old man grinned, folding his wrinkled face. He shook his finger in front of him. "The river is going to flood, Javi."

Javi squinted at the river, and Ian followed suit. Indeed, he could see water growing in the distance.

"It's okay," Javi said. "The water coming this far will be good for the soil."

Papá stopped smiling and shrugged his shoulders. "Maybe, maybe not. It's a lot of water."

Ian stepped in front of them and watched the river transform. The old man was right—there was a lot of water. It was growing and piling; it had begun to fold on itself and stack, and as it did so, the earth vibrated, and the train's sound grew.

Javi spoke quickly. "Papá, have you seen the river flood before?"

"Oh, yes, of course. Many times." He remained perfectly still while the water accelerated up, dragging the train's song along with it. "I think the key is to just let it flow over you, then forget about it. Or just avoid it."

Both Javi and Ian gazed in disbelief. The river had grown from a simple stream to something otherworldly, a massive growing vertical entity, expanding even on a dry summer day.

It had become a tower of water, unbelievably tall, unbelievably dense.

"It's quite magnificent, don't you think?"

Papá scratched his chin. "Maybe, but dangerous. I prefer quiet days."

Javi was mesmerized. He was watching the birth of something great, something ready to swallow them. His eyes glowed with a mix of wonder and worry, hope and fear. He wanted the world; he starved for it.

"It flooded when I was much younger," Papá said. "Did no good for me, but to be fair, I turned out okay."

"I see," Javi whispered.

"I guess you're different too," Papá said with a smile. "You'll always keep dreaming. Just the way some people go."

Javi turned to him. Even in his advanced age, Papá could still hold the face of a young father. Somewhat wise and somewhat uncertain all at once. "Okay, Papá," he said.

As the two shared their moment, Ian faced the water. It screamed toward them as a wave, shrieked as metal, shook the earth as an earthquake, and declared itself the victor of the universe. It came so quickly, but in its waters, Ian could have sworn he saw something, something exhilarating. The face of a woman. She gazed down at them, walking forward with the water as a bluish-green towering goddess, beckoning for them, welcoming them to her world.

Then the thought vanished and was replaced by Javi's passion, which filled the dream. In the second before the crash, Ian saw through Javi's eyes and experienced his hope, his nervousness, and his ambition all at once. He became enraptured by his pure optimism. Javi yearned for the world; he saw its beauty and potential. Wrapped in the euphoria of possibility, they had elation as the wave came. There were unlimited paths, unlimited opportunities, unlimited time, unlimited goals, and it was all there, right there, right in front of them, all for the taki——

The sensation ended. The sea swallowed the three of them and plunged them into an unknown darkness.

CHAPTER THIRTEEN

"Where did you go yesterday?"

Ian watched the floor. "Errands."

"Errands?" Oscar demanded. "What errands?"

"I don't know—eggs, milk. That sort of thing."

Oscar slapped his desk and kicked the floor. "Stop giving me bullshit. You can't just leave in the middle of the day without telling anybody."

Ian said nothing.

"Look at me!"

Ian saw a disrupted, aggravated, and annoyed face. Oscar's eyes were sharp, and his patience was gone.

"I've tried to help you, Ian, I really have. I've only tried to help you. But you obviously don't care. What do you want me to do?" He sighed and collapsed into his chair.

Ian defocused. He spotted his isolated tree on the corner of the street. The snow around it had all melted away.

"This status quo just isn't going to work, Ian." Oscar stared intensely at his pupil. "Are you going to step up or not?"

"I... I don't know."

"Isn't that the problem?"

The two shared an uneasy silence, which slowly slid into an uncomfortable conclusion. Ian's guts told him he should care, but his heart told him nothing, and his mind was entirely elsewhere.

"Ian, Ian. Ian. Ian! Are you going to get this fixed?"

Ian locked his gaze on the world outside. "Get what fixed?"

"'Get what fixed?'" Oscar stood right back up. "I mean, when are you going to wake up? When are you going to take things seriously?"

Ian felt an itch start to wrap itself around his body, an invisible rash infecting his cells.

"You must know I've been looking out for you. But I've watched you too long. You don't know what you're doing. You don't know up from down."

Up from down? War drums began to chant, bang, blast, and boom in his torso. *Don't know up from down?*

"I think I know *exactly* what's up and what's down," declared Ian.

"Oh yeah? How's that?"

He could barely hear him past the blood pumping through his ears. "I know what really matters."

"Is that so? What's that?"

Frustrated, he could only muster, "Not this."

"Huh, well, that's real helpful. Nice job, good observation, excellent thinking." Oscar laughed, then clicked his tongue. "Do you remember what I asked you to do before?"

Ian clenched his jaw. "Figure out what I wanted?"

"Yes. Do you know why I asked that?"

Ian mechanically pulled his neck side to side.

"I wanted you to figure out that sometimes in life, you need to work. You just need to. It isn't going to be easy. Clearly you didn't learn that."

Blood boiled in his brain, bile bubbled in his belly. *No more of this.* He rose.

"What are you doing?"

Ian turned around and approached the door.

"Fine, have it your way. Just get out. Get out of my office. Go!"

Ian took long, slow strides down the hall. Each step ached like magma flowed under him, incinerating his feet. Nothing was right. The anger wasn't cooling, only getting hotter.

When he passed the corner, he punched the gray wall.

"FUCK!"

A self-made bullet drove a stabbing pain into his hand, which cascaded down into his arm. He reeled back and clutched his hand against his chest. Half of his body stung. His knuckles were bright red and bloodied, unable to fully stretch open. Ian hoisted the dead hand and carried on. He could hear footsteps flooding the floor. The first one to arrive was Rohan.

Rohan ran straight to him. "Yo, man, you all right?"

"I'm fine." Ian tried to hurry past him, still clutching his busted hand.

Rohan tapped him on the shoulder. "Do you need to go to the hospital?"

Ian shoved his shoulder back, throwing Rohan to the other side of the hall. "I *said* I'm fine."

After Rohan slammed against the wall and slid to the floor, he yelled, "What's wrong with you?"

Ian ignored him and dragged himself to his desk. He could feel the weight of all their eyes on him. They burned into him, cut into his skin, but he wouldn't let them get past his bark. He refused to give them even a glance.

He reached for his coat with his working hand but lost his balance and stumbled to the floor. His body was failing him, collapsing under his pain, exhaustion, and anxiety. He lay there, half curled for a moment, while he felt their shadows come over him.

They whispered:

"Ian?"

"Should we call an ambulance?"

"Maybe the police."

He took one long, agonized breath and pushed himself up. He threw his coat over his shoulder and marched out to the elevators. There he slammed the down button, punching it twice with a fist.

He tried to resist looking while he waited for the elevator, but he couldn't. When it finally arrived, he took a final glance at the office. Everyone was staring at him, transfixed. They had gathered in a makeshift huddle to watch how his spectacle would play out. *I am their monkey*, he thought, *and they are their own fools.*

He entered the empty elevator and pressed the lobby button. After the door closed, he let himself slip down to its shining floor and held his pained hand in his lap.

AFTER IAN HAD CARRIED himself out of the office, he found the nearest empty bench, one at the end of the street. He limped toward it and, upon arrival, collapsed onto it. His torso fell down like deadweight, while his legs floated off its edge, limp. He tucked his injured hand into his pocket. The pain had hardened and turned into a dull throb.

His body was so hot he could barely sense the cold. He unzipped his jacket and unbuttoned the top of his shirt, letting his fever heat dissipate into the City.

Lying on the bench, he watched pedestrians march up and down the street, all in a rush to find a new final destination. Occasionally he would catch one of them glancing at him, but mostly they ignored him. He laughed. *They've become so inoculated by living they can't even see what's right in front of them.*

Staring at the sky, he considered his options. The sky wasn't too bad, he decided. Other than one definite patch of thick gray, it was clear. He pulled out his phone and opened the conversation with Belle and wrote: *I need to talk to you ASAP.*

Yes, the sky isn't too bad at all. He watched clouds drift above him, moving at random, then he closed his eyes.

He wanted rest, peace, to fall asleep, but it proved impossible. Even while blinded, his senses were overwhelmed; the shuffle and bustle of countless streetwalkers filled his ears, and the City's smoke filled his lungs. He couldn't tune them out. They were all screaming, getting louder and louder, unable to control themselves. The hustle of humanity had become too much, too foolish. He opened his mouth to shout, to scream, but then he felt a buzz above his stomach.

He peeled his eyes open and checked his phone. It read: *I'm free after 6. Don't be early. I'm at 68th and 5th Ave. Apt G20.*

Ian exhaled and allowed himself a small smile. His hand began to feel better. He stretched his fingers and pushed himself up, trotting forward with an uneven gait, throwing loose legs in front of him. He knew his destiny; he could see it. Down in the distance, past rows of skyscrapers, was the park.

Racing block by block, he retraced the dreams in his mind, filling his lungs with their vapors, and spread them throughout his bloodstream.

A laugh born as a chuckle evolved into a howl, and his glee was unleashed. *I've been a blind man, but soon maybe I'll be able to see.* Within their dreams, he could understand these people, better than they could even understand themselves.

The flare. The church. He decided Regi was an indecisive fool.

The stone. The birth of a city. Lizzy was scared and naive.

The collapse. The shadow man. The river. Adriana was an old woman racing toward the edge of the void.

But Belle and Javi! *Belle and Javi.*

Their names were sweet in his mouth; they sung like

ascending songbirds waking a bear from hibernation. *Javi and Belle.*

They rested above the earth, they stared down at the blue planet, they sent their love trickling into the atmosphere. *Belle and Javi.*

They rotated around each other as perfect binary stars; a constant gravity threw each into the arms of the other. *Javi and Belle.*

Their love showed potential, a pure power of passion that Ian had lost, or perhaps never had. And Javi. Oh, Javi. Javi's smile could cure his wounds, he knew. Javi's hopefulness, his vitality, were undeniable inspirations, marking everything that Ian was not and starved for.

Block by block, the dreams became his salvation. Any anxieties: Hallie, work, the City's weight, the past's pains, the future's uncertainty, Adriana's corrosion—they could all be erased. A simple explanation, a path to follow, a story from a single good dream could bring balance. All gaps in emotion could be filled, all stressors dismissed. The secrets of their dreams would soon give him the truths he sought and the guidance he needed and would make him whole.

There!

There was the park. Ian turned back around and absorbed the streets behind him, the people trailing him, and the cars stuck in traffic. He dismissed them all.

5:15 p.m. Soon he would see her.

He checked papernow.com one more time. It was as it was before, unchanged. Of course it was.

5:30 p.m. How could he keep waiting?

He watched a video, someone screaming into a camera about something he didn't care about.

5:45 p.m. What would Javi and Belle think of him?

Twilight came so early to the City, where the late sun was blocked early by man's towers.

6:00 p.m.

In front of Ian was a fantastic building, an architectural masterpiece of white columns and painted windowsills. It overlooked the park and stood on the dividing line between nature and man. Grand, giant, great! Colossal, classic, cultured!

Truly, he saw a brilliant beauty.

He had arrived.

GOLD CHANDELIERS, glossy marble, and immaculate mirrors circled the lobby, revealed by particles of light bouncing from wall to wall, sourced from burnt coal hundreds of miles away. They enveloped the doorman, who sat in the center of the lobby. Ian walked past him, heading to the elevator.

"Who are you here to see?" the doorman asked.

Ian continued.

"Excuse me."

Ian stopped and turned. "Sorry. I didn't see you there. Belle... Belle Miller. I'm here to see Belle."

The doorman peered at Ian. "Wait there a second."

He picked up his phone and clicked a button. "There's someone in the lobby for you. Okay. Yeah." Once more, he furrowed his brow. "Okay. G20."

Ian trotted forward, tripped on his left foot, and stumbled to the elevator. He smashed the up button and glanced back at the doorman. The doorman was still staring at him.

Fortunately the elevator came quickly, and Ian immediately found its corner upon entering. It carried him up, up, and up. He ascended through the building and nervously clicked his phone on and off. He checked his destination again: G20.

Up he went... 10... 11... 12... 14... Closer and closer... 18... 19... 20.

The hallway was claustrophobic, armed with dim light and

tight walls, but he had no fear. He tiptoed down the hall, supporting himself using the wall, and found the G.

A sudden dizziness hit him, a wave of vertigo, but then it went away. After a breath, a panic, a calm, and a resolution, he readied himself and pressed the bell.

"Coming!" Her voice hadn't changed a bit. It was Belle.

Ian ran over all the questions he had, every inch of every dream.

Why the brown dress? He could hear her footsteps.

Why did your teeth fall out? She was close.

How did you meet Javi? This was the moment.

What are you so scared of?

She cracked the door open just enough to allow her voice to come through, but not enough so that they could see each other. "What do you want?" she asked.

"I'm here to talk to you."

"About what? Are you a missionary? Or do you want money? I don't have either."

"No."

Ian stepped forward and pushed slightly on the door. She pulled back, and the two met eyes. She was older, significantly older, than the woman he had seen trying on dresses or eating lunch with her father or crawling out of rivers. She had disguised it fairly well, with a mix of makeup, hair dye, and fillers, but he could see through her mask with ease. He had the perfect reference point; all he knew of her were dreams of an earlier time.

Belle had examined him as well, and by her expression, she found herself more pleased with the results.

"Well, I didn't expect to be greeted by such a young *gentleman.*" She opened the door and waved him in. "Come in. I'll bring you some water."

With trepidation, he entered. Inside there was a long dining table with a sheet of glass as its top. Farther back, in her living room, Persian rugs and wide couches accompanied a massive black television that stretched from wall to wall, and to Ian's left was an open kitchen, which Belle strolled into.

"Take a seat," she called out, so he sat next to her dining table. He examined the back of the apartment, beyond the edge of her living room, where impressive windows lined her wall. They painted a dramatic picture of the park below, capturing the barren trees' sway and their flickering shadows during twilight's descent.

Then he spotted a shelf with pictures next to the table and hopped forward in his seat.

The first image he saw depicted a stranger boy, a stranger girl, a stranger man, and Belle. They posed, smiling together. Other images were solo shots of the children, but no one he recognized.

"You like the pictures?"

Ian zipped back to her.

She stood over him, holding a cup with an arm that stretched out of a sleeveless dress. With some hesitation, he took the cup. She had old black marks dotting her arm, which began in her elbow and ended in the middle of the forearm.

After he took the water, she slid down into the seat beside him.

"So what can I do for you?" Her voice was bubbly, forcibly pitched higher than what he remembered from her dreams. It seemed her every word was gilded with the thinnest shade of gold possible, a layer so thin it may as well have not been there at all.

His stomach twisted as he came to realize that *this was the moment.*

He exhaled. "I have some questions—"

"Do you want some music?" Belle interrupted. She stood up and walked to the kitchen. "I always have music going."

"No, that's all right, I'm fine."

"Listen to this." She tapped a gray box on the kitchen countertop, and the room became filled with soft, smooth instrumentals aligned together in a calm repetitive tune. "There, that's better."

"I wanted to ask about Javi," Ian spat out.

Belle raised an eyebrow, like he had just asked if it was morning at midnight. Then she corrected her form. "Oh, yes, yes. That's what you texted me about. Give me one second. I'll grab some wine from the kitchen. I usually drink a little bit around this time. You know it helps you fall asleep?"

He sighed and returned to the pictures. They each reflected a refined family: the children were well fitted, the man wore suits, and Belle wore silk dresses. That was the case for all except one, the one which managed to capture Ian's attention.

It was a picture of Belle as a girl with a woman beside her who wore a great number of bracelets and a man on her other side who wore an unbuttoned shirt. They all were stacked together, laughing in one great heap on the couch, while they turned in shock toward an unanticipated camera flash.

"Here," Belle said as she handed Ian a glass filled with red wine.

Annoyed, he took it. "Do you always give strangers wine?"

She laughed. "I don't get many visitors. And besides…" She smirked. "I don't get many *visitors*."

He spun the glass, watching the liquid swirl. He hadn't drunk in a while. He took a sip. It couldn't hurt. Maybe it could help.

Belle sat back down and leaned against the table. "Anyways," she said. "What were you asking about?"

"Javi."

"Ah, yes!" She looked up and grinned. "What a great summer!"

Ian leaned forward. "What do you mean, 'a great summer'?"

She rose a finger and took a deep sip of her drink.

"I have a lot of questions," said Ian.

She swallowed her fill and put the cup down. In a shrill voice, she squeaked, "Me too!"

He watched her teeth flash up and down with every expression. They were flawlessly, perfectly white. He raised his voice and said, "Listen, I really need your help."

"Oh, is that so?" She leaned forward. "Usually it's the other way around, but that's okay! How can I help you?"

"The summer."

"Oh yes, the summer!" She took another sip. "It was so long ago. Wow, what a time! It really does fly fast."

"What does?"

"Time." She looked at Ian and spoke like a child. "Do I look older than forty?"

"What? No."

"Good. Right answer." She laughed. "Like I said, it was a great summer. I was in my later twenties then. You can do the math. I had recently obtained this quaint little apartment around midtown. I was getting a renovation done for the kitchen, and one day, in walked this crew."

She took another sip.

"And in the crew there was this one man, who, I must be honest with you..." She looked at Ian. "What is your name?"

"Ian."

"Ah, Ian! I must be honest with you, Ian, this one man in the crew was fantastic. He was handsome, strong, and turned out to be very sweet."

"So that was Javi?" he asked with a trace of awe.

She grinned and nodded. "Yes, Javi! So, Javi was around quite often, and at the time I was between jobs and relationships, so I was around quite often as well. His English wasn't the best, but his accent made more than up for it. And he tried so hard."

With a mock accent, she said, "*Thank you, Miss Belle. We're almost done, Miss Belle.*" She looked to the side and waved as if dismissing the memory. "It was very cute."

"So he worked on your kitchen?"

"Yes, that's what I said!" she snapped. "Isn't it?"

He flinched and said slowly, "Yes, you did. You did say that."

"Good." She took a sip, smiled again, and laughed. "I thought I must've said something else. Anyways, they did a great job, and when they were finishing up, I told him I wanted to see him more." She concentrated her gaze at Ian. "I must say, we became quite the item."

Ian tapped his foot. He looked at his own drink and took a gulp.

"I couldn't have him at my place, since my parents were around so often, checking up on me, hating on him, so I visited him. And I must tell you, his first place was terrible. Awful. Imagine this: five men living on the floor on cots, in one room. Horrible. I couldn't have it, so I rented him a cheap apartment and bought him a whole new set of furniture."

Ian spilled out all his words at once. "Was the apartment right by a subway station? Did you buy him a mattress?"

Belle took a sip and scratched her head. "Well, yes, I bought him a mattress, a bed, and a bunch of other things. And you're right! It was right by a train platform. It was so annoying; the train woke me up almost every night." She refilled her cup. "You impress me, Ian! So intuitive. Here," she said as she reached out to fill his glass.

"I'm okay."

"I insist!" she insisted, so he watched his glass be filled to the brim. He took a sip.

"So, you two were together?"

"Yes, and it was a fantastic summer! He worked while, honestly, I lounged a bit. I vacationed in France, I came back, I visited him, and I bid my time. I had lost a job, so I had plenty of time. Listen to this, Ian." She stood up and clutched the air like there were two invisible handlebars. "You see, he had been riding a bike everywhere, *swoosh, swoom.*"

She plopped back down and stretched her arm out across the table toward Ian. "Imagine that. A grown man riding around all day on a bicycle. *Ridiculous.* He couldn't afford the subway, so I gave him money for the train. He was so thankful. '*Thank you, Belle!*' That's how he would say it. '*Thank you, Belle!*'" She took a sip. "Great times."

Ian found his words carefully. "That's very interesting. So that summer, when you were together, did you have any interesting dreams?"

With a forced daintiness, she put her glass down and made a curious face. "I don't know, maybe. What kind of dreams, Ian?" She tucked her fist under her chin and stared up at him. He moved an inch back.

"Uh... like dreams about buying a dress, and the credit card not working... Or maybe a dream where your teeth fell out?"

For three impossibly long seconds, Belle glared at him coldly, finally without a response. It seemed she was about to say something but then shook it out of her mouth. Instead she raised her head and laughed. "Oh, you are such a strange one, Ian! Drink up, drink up. You need to cool your head."

"Just tell me first: did you have those dreams?"

She took a sip. "Maybe, maybe not. Like I said, it was a long time ago."

"What about Adriana, did you talk to her?"

She looked at Ian, puzzled. "Who?"

"Javi's sister!"

Immediately, Belle pointed at her temple. "Ah, yes, I remember her, Adriana. *Adri*! Not my favorite, that's for sure!"

"What do you mean, 'not your favorite?'"

"Well, first of all, she was a real damper in general. She was always telling Javi that he had to stop seeing me. And she called me nasty names! I swear, Ian, she was a real piece of work. See, I never asked how either of them got here... but I very easily could have got her sent back if I wanted to. *Easily*." She took a sip. "But, I never did. Never even brought it up! I even helped her out."

"Why was she trying to break you guys up?"

Belle gave an exaggerated sigh. "Well, I did have a tiny problem that summer."

"What problem?"

"I had a tiny, tiny drug problem." She waved it off. "It really was no big deal, trust me, and I got over it eventually, but that woman always would whine in her voice, '*You, no good! No good!*'" Belle rolled her eyes. "Her English was terrible."

"So what happened to you and Javi?"

Belle paused for a moment and took another sip. "Well, all summers have to come to an end."

Ian held on to the edge of the table. "Where is he? Can I talk to him?"

She turned to him and laughed. Her eyes glowed. "Actually, he's here!"

"He's *here*?" exclaimed Ian.

She smiled and nodded. "Yes, he's in my room. Let me grab him."

She stood and strolled off, and Ian's head began pounding once again. This woman was useless, he had decided, but maybe he could get some answers from Javi, some explanations, some advice.

Belle yelled out from her hallway, "If you need more wine, feel free to pour some more!"

"Okay," he whispered. He took a final gulp and scrunched up into a ball. He leaned his head against the table and stared at his shoes while he took deep breaths in and out. All the pieces were coming together, albeit in a confused pattern. Maybe once he spoke to Javi, he would begin to feel better.

"Coming!" Belle shouted.

This was the moment. He heard footsteps emerging and heard another shout, "Here he is!"

Ian looked up, and everything in his body stopped.

She held an urn.

It was beautiful, painted with rich white gloss and sharp black and red stripes that crisscrossed down its side, coming together in a pattern only the greatest artisans could achieve. Its top covering was a solid piece of pure silver splashed with flecks of gold decorating its upper rim. Truly it may have been one of the most beautiful things he had ever seen. Impressively functional too, considering it could encapsulate an entire life.

Belle held it out in front of her. "Here!" she said with a smile. "Do you want to hold it?"

Ian's mouth hung open. "I... I... I..."

She sat down and carefully placed the urn aside on the far end of the table. "Oh." She touched the top of his hand. "You didn't know? Oh, wow, it must've been twelve years ago now."

All he could muster was a weak shake of his head. His legs were giving out; he was falling into the chair.

"I assumed all of Javi's friends knew," she said plainly. "He overdosed."

Ian's head throbbed and banged. He shook it back and forth; the disorienting pain from the early dreams had returned.

"It was the worst thing ever," she whined. "The train woke me up the next day, like I told you, and he was next to me! It was terrible! I'll never unsee it, Ian, *never*. He had choked on his own vomit."

She took a sip. "It was everywhere, all over the sheets, all over me! It smelled so bad…" She took another sip. "I had vomited a bit too, to be honest, but it turned out I was fine, thank god, just a headache and some chest pain! I had to call 9-1-1 and everything. I paid for the funeral. It was a small affair, only me and Adri went. Get this—I was crying, of course, but she still yelled at me. She even started hitting me."

Ian grabbed the rest of his wine and poured it down.

"I felt bad for her. Really, Javi was all she had. No one else could tolerate her, and she was basically broke, so I offered to let her move into his old apartment, and she said, '*no*,' but then eventually she said, '*sí*.'" She took another sip, then raised her voice. "You know, that's the issue with these people. Takers. They're all takers. I even paid for her when she got Alzheimer's, the poor bitch."

The moon, the earth, the river flashed before Ian. He saw it all. He saw the joy in the man and the boy. This moment couldn't be real. It couldn't be. Ian decided none of it could be real. He could only shake his head.

"You know, he would always say, '*I love you, I love you so much*.'" Belle sighed again and spoke softer. "I could never tell if he was just in it for the money or if he just started to like the drugs, but I wanted to believe it, you know?"

She finished her glass. "Well, I sure stopped taking hard drugs after that. No more speedballs for me! Anyways, how did you know Javi? You're so young!"

Ian weakly lifted his chin to meet her gaze. Her eyes had grown wet, barely able to hold back a stream of tears.

He tried to stand. "I… I need to go," he muttered.

"Oh no, no, no." Belle grabbed his hand and tugged him down, back to his chair. "The night has just begun! Stay for a bit." She slid her hand up his arm, then pushed him back onto his chair.

Ian ran his hands through his hair. "I really got to go."

He refocused and felt a sudden heat. Belle had snaked even

closer to him. "Ian, my ex has the kids for the rest of the week," she said in hurried words. "You don't need to go."

Ian stared at her. Her face seemed like a ghastly apparition, a poor attempt at disguising a tired illness. Her cheeks were sunken, void of life or substance. She had nothing, she was lost, and she knew it. Something had been hollowed out of her long ago.

And he saw his reflection in her eyes.

He made his final attempt to stand. He knew if he fell, there would be no getting up.

His muscles did not seem up to the task. His body shook under his weight; his cinder-block feet glued him to the floor.

He began to tip.

Terror struck his heart. It informed him that he was certain to fail. Everything was spinning, everything was in a crumble. The weight of countless lives collapsed on top of him. The world pulled him down, pulled him all the way down, and he knew it was over. He swayed and bent over, preparing for a crash. He nearly closed his eyes, but before he fell, as he dipped and rotated, he caught another glimpse of the urn.

No, he thought, *I need to leave.*

Neurons reignited in his brain and flares rocketed across his cranium. He grunted, punched his chest, and shoved himself back up.

After a final shiver, he had stabilized.

Standing straight, he took slow, measured steps toward the door. He whispered to himself, "I need to go."

"Please!" Belle reached out and grabbed his hand and cried, "Stay!"

Ian turned around. He recoiled at her face, took a final glance at the urn, and said, "He was beautiful... and you poisoned him."

Then he left.

. . .

Ian wobbled down the sidewalk, barely able to maintain his balance. On occasion, he grabbed the nearest decrepit building wall or rusty street sign to stabilize. Nothing seemed to work right—not his legs, not his arms, and especially not his mind.

He pulled out his phone multiple times to jitter with its power button. He turned it off, on, off, on, off, on, using it more as a pacemaker than anything else. Twilight had firmly faded into night, leaving only darkness to feast on the City, but in his state, it made no difference to him, night or day. He could barely see, he could barely think, so he let the blunt light of streetlamps be his guide.

With each step forward, he brought himself further inward, further inside his dizzy head. He wasn't sure how long he had been walking when he came to a hazy decision, but he knew he could not go any further.

He pushed himself against a cold wall and held his phone with a shaky hand. He raised it in front of his eyes, letting it burn his corneas.

First, after he blinked out the pain, he summoned a ride. Then, with no thinking at all, he opened up his chat with Hallie.

He reread her last message: *Hallo! How you doing?*

How was he doing?

He tapped out: *Hallie, can you meet me? I really need to see you*

He waited, staring at his phone for a minute, anticipating a response, but none came. Soon his car arrived, and he dragged himself inside.

Neither he nor the driver uttered a word, or even a sound. They cruised through the City in an unusual quiet, with only a single ambulance wailing far away. Rolling block by block, their entertainment consisted of the temporary glows of lampposts that came and went. Ian used each gleam as a signal to check his phone, but each time he checked, he still did not have an answer.

They had moved too fast. Within minutes, his apartment building, his towering torturer, materialized only a street away. He didn't want to go back; he didn't want to be there alone.

The driver ignored his unsaid fears and refused to relent. The car stopped, and Ian silently crawled out its back and dumped himself in front of his stoop. There he stood, shivering, waiting, anticipating, while the night's cold nudged him forward. He ambled up, swaying with every step as he clutched onto the guard rails for dear life. At the top of the stairs, in front of the building's door, he hesitated once more. He reached for his phone again and finally called her.

It rang seven times. She did not answer. He ended the call before he could leave a message.

Inside, he used his phone's light to find his way up a dark staircase, back to the tiny cube that composed his apartment. Outside its door, he waited, staring at its gray paint. He could feel the wine flowing freely in his blood. Everything spun, wobbled, teetered. Then he leaned over and used his body weight to push himself in. It wasn't locked anyways.

The room seemed so strange. During the night everything took on some form of disguise. Dirty plates became clean when left unseen in cloudy sinks. Messy clothes could be pushed under the bed and not even be noticed. The furniture in particular took on a dreadful stillness in the dark. Each piece suddenly became foreboding and unwelcoming, as if the day's light had been the only thing keeping them awake, and now they were not to be disturbed. Alone in the night, the room's sole source of motion became Ian's slim shadows. They shifted as he walked in, fueled by trace ambient light from outside his window.

He fell back onto his bed and ripped off his shirt. He crawled onto his mattress and wrapped himself in a blanket, moaning and shivering. He couldn't tell if his body had frozen or if the room's heat wasn't working. He just knew he was cold.

Inside his cocoon, he made his decision once more. He pulled his phone up his chest and called Hallie again.

It rang long enough to give time for his heart to sink, but just before it rang a final time, he heard her voice. "Hello, Ian? What is it?"

He nearly cried. Each word arrived like a delicious drop of water after years in a desert.

"Hallie," he slurred, "can you meet me at my place?"

She did not respond initially, only gave dead silence over the phone. Then she burst. "What? You don't talk to me for a month, and now you suddenly ask me over? Sorry, goodbye."

"Stop."

She did not speak, but she also did not hang up. He knew she was listening; he could still hear her soft breath over the line. "Please. Come over. I just need... someone."

Slowly, she asked, "What's wrong? Are you okay?"

"I'll send the address. Please just come. I just need to see you."

He waited, waited forever, until he heard a reluctant, "Fine."

He sighed. "Thank you." He hung up, sent her the address, and clutched his phone once more.

He twisted in his bed while silence returned and flooded over him. He considered watching a video, but even that effort didn't seem worth it. Instead, he squirmed.

He rocked back and forth, side to side, until he settled on staring at the ceiling. He could feel his body slowly sinking into the mattress and knew sleep was not far, but fortunately the ceiling proved to be a worthy distraction. In the late night, it appeared enchantingly gloomy.

Limited light from outside mixed with its white paint to make a perfect shade of gray, a clean canvas on which he could paint any and everything. Refining his palette, an occasional neon or car ray would dribble through the window and bounce throughout the room, splashing rare strokes of color onto his monochrome imagination.

He could see it all in the ceiling. Moments danced either as shifting shadows, real and imagined, or as flashes of light from the street, coming and quickly going.

There was Javi, there was Adriana, there was Belle. They tussled with one another in love, hate, and fear before they left entirely.

There was Regi and Lizzy together. Their relationship held like a quivering string pulled too far, ready to snap. Dreams didn't change so quickly, Ian knew. Their marriage wouldn't last. They had remained together only for the child; stability was an impossibility.

There was Oscar, smashing his fists on his desk, unable to find peace with Ian or himself.

There were Rohan and Zoey happily marching in a circle, without hesitation. How jealous Ian was of them.

And there were the pains of the past he had buried but could never really forget.

They were all there, on his ceiling, walking with the City's shadows. He could see all the infinite moments, dream and wakefulness, tussling and tugging at each other in a torrent of confusion. The urn and the boy. The stone and the mother.

Do they not see what I see?

They must, he decided. How could they not? It was their lives after all, *their dreams*. Even in the dark, perhaps *especially* in the dark, it all became crystal clear.

In the midst of this eternity rapidly condensing itself into a solid and weighty conclusion, Ian was interrupted by a buzz, a shrill sound that shot through the silence of the room. He flinched.

He stretched the full length of his body to press the button to allow Hallie, his first house guest, in. After the buzz subsided, he pulled his shirt back on, retreated back into his bed, and sat up beside its mantle, all in a feeble attempt to project a shred of dignity.

His attempt failed. He kept sliding down, sliding back onto his bed, sliding where his body wanted him to be. He tried again. He was nearly out of time.

Knock-knock-knock.

"Come in!" cried Ian.

The door swung open, and Hallie walked in.

"THIS PLACE IS A WRECK."

Ian glanced around the room. She was right. Upon her arrival, everything that had once been hidden became plainly revealed. Clothes spilled out from under the bed. Partially filled cups rolled on the floor. Dirty plates were stacked out of the sink.

"Can I turn on the light?" she asked.

Ian did not respond, so she turned it on anyway.

The bright white burned. He grabbed his eyes and shut them tight.

"Please," he said in a croaked voice, "leave it off. Just open the window or something."

"Fine."

Once he felt the heat dissipate from his eyelids, he blinked and cracked his eyes open.

"So what's up?"

Under his window, she sat in his lone chair and stared at him. Above her were no stars, only tall buildings and a thin moon which illuminated her face. It annoyed him how good she looked, how the dark only made her radiance even more pronounced. After everything that had happened, her presence didn't even seem real, perhaps just another dream.

But she had come. She was there.

Ian exhaled heavily. "I've been searching, Hallie."

Hallie crossed her arms. "For what?"

"I'm not quite sure, but at the same time, I'm very sure. Come to think of it, I remember this one dream I had when I was a kid where I was falling and couldn't stop. I'd go down, down, down but never hit the bottom; there was never a crash. Eventually I'd just drift awake before I hit the bottom. This feels a little like that."

"Ian," Hallie demanded, "what are you talking about?"

"It's amazing that I still remember it after all this time."

She raised her voice. "Have you been drinking? I think you may have had a little too much."

"That might be true, but lots of things are true." Ian nodded to himself. "Yes, in fact, take this, for instance—I met someone very much like you. An old friend, a dreamer, someone who sees the world wide open."

Hallie gave a small laugh. Ian couldn't tell if she was nervous or had finally embraced the absurdity of the situation. "Is that what you think of me?"

He smiled a wild grin. "Well, isn't it true? Let me say this, Hallie, Hallie... Hallie. I think I love you, Hallie. Yes, yes, I do! I love you, Hallie. I think about you all the time. I see you all of the time. You're there, right there—right there out of the corner of my eye on every street, on every screen I see. So much has happened, so much has been spoiled, except you. I think it's true: I love you."

Hallie frowned, sighed, then weakly scoffed. "Even if a part of that were true, you don't love me, Ian. You may be *in love* with me, but you don't love me."

Ian looked at her, flabbergasted. "What's the difference?"

Hallie slowed her speech and stressed every syllable. "If you're in love with someone, you can very easily *fall out* of love. When you love someone, there's no room for uncertainty, and honestly, right now you seem very uncertain about pretty much everything."

He placed his hands on his face and cradled his sinking head. "Damnit, Hallie."

He knew she was right, of course, but her casual accuracy only made his drunkenness worse, more agitated and belligerent.

He began again. "You have different eyes than me, both of you do. Well, he *did*. You see everything brighter, you see the heart in everyone."

"What does that mean?"

Ian opened his eyes and tapped on his chin, acting pensive, but he did not need to think, for the words came freely. "It means you breathe while I choke. You hear while I go deaf. You see while I'm blind. Or maybe it's the other way around. Yes, actually, yes, *it is* the other way around! I see *too much*, and you've got some mighty blinders on."

"What the hell are you talking about, Ian?"

Ian clapped his hands together. "Like I said before, I've been searching. Yes, I've been searching in skyscrapers, I've been searching in trees. I've been searching in streets, I've been searching in strangers. Do you understand?"

She sighed. "No, Ian, I don't."

How can she not understand? "It's like this—I've been searching in the day, I've been searching at night. I've been searching in your eyes, I've been searching in phones. I've been hunting for answers, brawling for explanations." As he spoke, he raised his voice until it growled and his body rocked. "I only wanted some whys, some whats, maybe a few whens, a little direction, a bit of inspiration, a friend, a story, something to keep me going. I've been searching everywhere, through everything, through everyone. Through their damn memories, through their awful dreams! And you know what I found, Hallie?"

Hallie, half entranced, half terrified, whispered, "What?"

"Dust. Dust and disappointment."

The words fell like an anchor and killed the conversation.

He had no more to say, and based on Hallie's expression, she did not know what to say.

But she also looked like she *wanted* to say something, and eventually, she found her courage. "Ian, I know you're very drunk, and I know you're upset, and I know this'll be hard to hear, but I'm not going to lie to you. You've got to be one of the dumbest people I've ever met."

Ian raised an eyebrow. "What?"

"What are you looking for? It's clear you were never going to find it, and even if you had found something like it, you wouldn't have been satisfied. Seriously, man, what do you think you're missing? What do you want me to tell you? What do you want me to say? What do you want me to do? I have nothing to say, and there's nothing I can do. I'm sorry, but you've got to get your head out of your ass, out of the dirt, and get some self-awareness. Nothing's easy and for whatever you conjured me to be, know this: I'm no goddess."

He slumped into his bed and drowned under her words. She was right again, of course, but it did not help, not at all. It did not stop the horribleness from slipping in, and he could feel it coming again. It came under shadows, moved in silence, crept into stomachs, and infected heads. It had come to him so many times before, so many days and so many nights, and each time he had denied it, but still it had come, paralyzing him, freezing him, sucking the vitality out of his body until all he could do was lay in bed. It came as an unstoppable weight, dragging him down without remorse, and nothing could stop it now.

"Why did you originally talk to me?" he asked quietly.

"Where? What do you mean?"

"On the train. Why did you talk to me? I know you came up to me. We both know if you hadn't perched over me like some kind of hawk, I would've never approached you."

Hallie scratched her head. "I guess I thought you were a

little cute, and I was a little lonely, and I was tired of swiping strangers on my phone. And you seemed a little lonely too."

Silence resumed, until Ian groaned. "I can't sleep here."

"Why not?"

He hesitated. "My mattress gives me incredible dreams, but they all have led to an abyss."

Hallie groaned. "You really have drunk too much." Reluctantly, she made a proposition. "You can sleep on my couch if you really need to."

He crawled forward on his bed. "You have a couch?"

"Yes," Hallie said impatiently. "A couch and a roommate."

Ian pushed his fist under his head and looked up at Hallie. She had those otherworldly eyes again. Perhaps everything would be fine, a part of him reasoned, and perhaps his right brain even believed it. But his left brain knew the reality of their situation: they would not, could not, allow things to be *fine*.

The horribleness had metastasized in both cerebral hemispheres. In a sudden, sharp moment, when he gazed at her under his window, he hated everything. He hated how the moonlight shined on her face. He hated how beautiful she was. He hated the way she spoke as if she knew nothing, when she knew everything. He hated that she did not love him. He hated that she was happy. He hated her ability to craft green beanies. He hated that she could make things at all. And he hated that he hated her because he hated himself.

With a faint trace of venom in his voice, he said, "You must think I'm crazy, or maybe just a loser."

She shook her head. "No, I don't. I just think you need some rest."

"Rest," said Ian. "I don't think that's possible at this point. It's interesting. Your apartment must be pretty big to fit an entire couch. I can barely fit a chair here."

"What are you getting at?"

He inched up further. "You know, Hallie, we really haven't talked enough at all about each other. There's still so much I don't know. You're an artist, right? It must be pretty hard to afford an apartment in the city."

She glared at him. "I liked you better when you didn't talk. Now you start asking questions about me?"

"So do your parents pay for your apartment? Or does the pottery bring in any money?"

Hallie spoke with a slow, controlled voice. "It's sculptures. Right now I'm just taking classes."

He propped himself on his elbows and held his face in his hands. "Why sculptures? They break so easily."

"Seriously, Ian, you're starting to annoy me. Stop talking, you're drunk."

The spite came easy, spilling over from the boiling horribleness, flowing freely as a hot river, from blood to brain to tongue, and Ian found himself at the mercy of himself, unable to stop. "No, Hallie, I'm the most sober I've ever been. In fact, I'm sober enough to see what this is all about. I see you clearly. You're just here to make yourself feel better, to take up another pity project. You should learn—everything will eventually disappoint you. I guess I'm just a quicker study. There's nothing here for you."

Hallie raised her hands in exasperation and stood. "I came here because I was worried about you," she said shakily. "I have tried to help you, but clearly I was wrong to come at all. It's obvious that you're just an asshole."

Ian chuckled. "You know when I first saw you on the subway, I thought I saw something special, I really did. Now I see the truth: I saw nothing at all, just another face in the crowd."

She walked to the door.

"Now you're just going to leave? I guess I shouldn't be surprised."

She opened the door. "Bye, Ian." She slammed it behind her. And she was gone.

Ian let out a feral scream. He rustled in his bed but eventually locked himself in the fetal position. He held out for another minute until exhaustion finally did him in.

The sun seeped into Ian's skin, the grass shined green, and the soil was soft. Any grog that had lingered in his head before he fell asleep had been erased, replaced by clarity of mind. He could see better in dream, in the memory of an emotion, than in day. He could feel everything flowing with the breeze, a soft wind signaling the start of summer. He could feel peace on the earth as it turned slowly.

Great glass-and-steel edifices dotted the distant landscape, but he dismissed them. In the park's serenity, they were distant memories and nothing more.

He turned his focus toward the couple. They rested on a hill's peak, camouflaged under the shadow of a great oak. Gentle green leaves fluttered above their heads, and strong brown branches welcomed them with open arms. The day could not have been more perfect.

Belle stood while Javi was lying. He had fallen asleep, resting the top of his head by the tree's bark while Belle nervously paced on the edge of the shade, looking down the hill as if searching for someone.

The sum of it—the serenity, Javi, Belle, the grass—made

Ian uneasy. The combination was too rosy, too optimistic, given what he knew. He wanted to walk away and disappear, but he had nowhere to go except toward them.

Belle peeked down an empty gravel path at the base of the hill. She checked left, right, and glanced at where Ian stood. Then she turned around and ran to Javi; she had determined there was no one else, only her and her love and the joy of summer.

Ian could not tell if it was simply because she was the youngest that he had ever seen her, or if it was because of dream, but she held a vitality that she had lost. When she moved, it was almost as if she floated, hopping with light steps that barely touched the ground. Her dress drifted with the wind, and her hair followed. With an unmistakable yearning in her eyes, she ran to Javi.

She jumped on the grass beside him and crawled on his legs, nudging him awake. Javi shook himself out of his slumber, and she looked at him, and he looked at her.

She tugged at his jeans; he kissed her neck. Each caress sent particles of electricity bouncing throughout their bodies, spinning in all directions. She threw herself on top of him, and he held her with firm hands under her dress.

Ian wanted to look away, but something inside of himself didn't allow him to. Instead, he fell to his knees and dug his hands into the soil. Under the tree, they weaved into one another and out again. They became lost to the world but found each other. Ian felt the shake of their bodies, the earth, the train, the dream. He felt a rumble turn into a roar, and everything became one.

He felt the dirt beneath his fingers, and he felt Belle's hunger. He felt shockwaves exploding throughout her body and the warmth of the summer sky.

All she wanted was all of him.

Soon tears flowed down his face while his body throbbed

and his heart shuddered. He looked up at the pair, folding and disappearing within each other, their bodies intertwined. Then he looked further up, into the blue heavens, and said, "No more."

Ian received no response but the sound of Belle's ecstasy and the flow of summer wind and a train approaching. He turned his head to the ground and pushed his forehead against the soft soil, wishing the earth would swallow him whole. He shouted down where no one could hear him and waited until the shaking underneath him had grown unstoppable. The convulsions of the ground became a cataclysmic mix of passion and sound, reaching the point where Ian could no longer understand what was real and what was dream. Until, after an eternity, in a sudden explosion of darkness, everything ended.

He thought *it was all too cruel.*

CHAPTER FOURTEEN

I an awoke to pitch black darkness and shockwaves pulsating throughout his body. He jumped out of bed, tripped, smashed his right thigh against the hardwood floor, shouted, grabbed his leg, and pulled it close to him. After rubbing the wound, he crawled toward the bathroom.

Halfway there, he pushed himself up and limped. He used the wall as his crutch and recklessly threw himself forward. Once he felt tiled floor under his feet, he reached for the switch in the dark and flicked it on.

There was a moment of blindness, then clarity.

At long last, Ian stared into the mirror and faced himself. His eyes shifted wildly and carried deep bags underneath them. His skin had grayed and dried out, having soaked in his stress and weariness. His hair had bloated, become tangled and dirty, filthy and full of sweat.

He stumbled back, shocked by himself, but his gaze did not waver; he couldn't look away. He stared at the reflection of a stranger staring at him, someone he did not recognize or someone he simply refused to recognize. He saw a ghost.

He spat and let his head hang low over the sink, dragged

down by dreams mixed with memory. He turned on the faucet and let cold water pour down on his hair, trying to drown everything away. All these fears, hopes, passions, loves—he had become their keeper, and he hated it. They all had disappeared, vanished, and yet here he was, still remembering.

Slowly he pulled his head up and looked at himself again. He stewed over his deficiencies—the redness in his eyes, the sweat on his chest, the weakness in his heart—before he came to a final solution. He flicked the bathroom light off and dashed to his countertop.

He traced his hand against the marble and reached down and threw drawers open, rattling the entire room. Two dishes fell off their precarious stack and shattered on the floor. A shard grazed his shin. He winced and ignored the pain. He had something to find.

He reached into a drawer and thumbed the silverware. *There.* He pulled out the first knife he felt and held it close to his eye. Then he threw it across the room. It was too dull, too soft. It wouldn't be sharp enough.

Reaching back in, he found something that pricked his thumb. He pulled it out and nodded. It was a wide cooking knife with a wooden handle and a fresh, unused blade. Faint bits of outside light bounced off its stainless steel, making it gleam as he turned it. Then he tightened his spine and approached his bed.

First, he threw his blanket onto the floor. It was disgusting, a length of fabric drenched in sweat. Next, he grabbed his bedsheet by its corner and ripped it off, unveiling the bottom layer.

There it was, naked and exposed: *the mattress.*

He looked at the ugly thing, worn away, decayed. Its end was undeniable. It was time to put old matters to rest, to let old dreams find an eternal quiet. He decided now was its time to die.

Ian stabbed the mattress.

He was relentless, maniacal, attacking with frenetic energy. With every stroke, the yellow foam interior became exposed. It peeked out and then was pushed out by the raw force of his blows. He needed to attack every angle. Nothing could be left. Narrow cuts turned into wide tears, running throughout its soft surface. Eventually he changed his strategy and stabbed the knife deep into one corner and dragged it across to the other, then repeated the process with new angles, shredding the mattress, tearing it apart.

Finally, after a minute, he realized his arms were shaking and his body was aching. Hot sweat was dripping into his eyes and tears were rolling down his cheeks.

He stepped back and examined his work.

He had cut it down, down to its coils, and had even sliced through a few of them. Foam oozed out of its skin while other portions dipped and sagged. He paused for a moment, expecting something inside of him to change, to warm or cool off, but the sight brought him no peace.

The mattress was dead.

He dropped the knife, letting it clatter to the floor, and jumped onto the mess. One spring's cold steel pricked his back while raw foam rubbed against his head.

As its wrecked surface crumbled, he fell in and became absorbed by the mattress's remains. Before he reached its bottom, he stretched out and snatched his phone from his nightstand and squinted to see the time. 3:27 a.m.

He vigorously tapped and scrolled, jumping from image to image, from video to video, from moment to moment.

Papernow.com still had not been updated.

Another friend was engaged.

Forests were burning.

Politicians were fighting.

People were starving.

And ice was melting.

So many stories came in an unstoppable torrent, an overwhelming, chaotic mix of noise and anxiety. He searched and searched. He was looking for nothing in particular, just anything to take his mind off the body beneath his back.

In his journey, he stumbled upon an image. It had arrived in the world three days ago, full of color and light and passion. In it, Lizzy was lying on a bed holding something in a white towel. He zoomed closer and closer, until something inside of him stirred.

In her arms, she held a child. It barely existed, just a small ugly brownish-pink bald thing peeking out of its blanket with two sleepy eyes. But in the picture, it glowed, drawing all its onlookers' attention toward it. Even Ian could not deny its nature, given the way it gently wrapped its entire hand around Lizzy's pointer finger. It was so alive.

He took his phone and weighed it in his hand. It was solid, developed from fine engineering and design, a brilliant piece of glass. He launched it toward the wall.

Milliseconds later, the sound of the screen's shatter filled the room's silence. A great thump followed. Then the silence returned.

He groaned and cycled through his mind: Lizzy's anxiety, Regi's uncertainty, Adriana's withering, Belle's emptiness, and Javi. Javi. For Javi, there was only ash.

He came to a final conclusion: He understood them better than they understood themselves. Their relentless dreams were of no use. All of them were being carried by an unstoppable and indifferent train. Neither Oscar's nor Hallie's platitudes could subdue his hypothesis: they were all alone and going nowhere.

And that was the thought that churned in Ian's brain as he fell asleep.

✩ ✩ ✩ ✩ ✩

Ian watched himself walk down empty sidewalks, wandering under the shadows of skyscrapers, searching for some kind of relief, but he couldn't find anyone or anything. He searched and searched, probed and scoured the world for sound, and strayed to the middle of the street, but there were no cars to watch, nor any to block his path. The concrete jungle had gone barren, devoid of life, sound, or movement. Only his soft steps interrupted the complete stillness.

He looked up at the buildings whose glass windows let no light through. Instead they offered gray shadows, concealing their contents behind them. They were no grand structures, just uniform undefined rectangles of dull steel. And above everything, above Ian, above the earth, above the City, a single thick gray cloud clogged the sky.

With some curiosity, he asked himself, "Where am I going?"

Beside him, he heard a familiar voice. "Nowhere in particular."

Ian turned, and there was Javi. He strode with a grin on his face while he looked into the distance.

"What are you so happy about?" muttered Ian.

Javi offered a mild shrug of his shoulders and kept smiling.

Ian sighed, and the two walked in silence for a while. They walked straight, going block by block, building by building.

He kept looking for something novel, something colorful, a bright tower, perhaps a car or two, but there was nothing new at all. Growing impatient, he asked Javi, "Where are we going?"

"We're going straight."

Ian rolled his eyes. "I can see that."

Javi turned to Ian as they walked. "You ought to stop asking so many questions. That can get you into trouble."

"What's that supposed to mean?"

Javi stopped smiling. "It can be dangerous to get too deep inside your own head."

Ian sighed and waved his arms, gesturing to the landscape in front of him. "Look for yourself, Javier."

He laughed. "No one's called me that in ages."

Ian stopped, stood, and spoke to the ground. "There's nothing here, nothing at all."

Javi looked around. "I guess so. You're right."

Ian, disgusted, inched closer to Javi. "How can you be so casual?"

Javi shrugged again and kept walking, and Ian followed him.

"Look, Javi," he said. "you haven't seen what I've seen."

"Oh?" Javi asked. "What's that?"

Ian shivered, then said all at once, "Adriana is fading, Belle is empty, and you... You are dust!"

"True enough," Javi said, smiling.

The two walked in silence for a while after that. Occasionally Javi glanced up at the unremarkable buildings and down at the road, while Ian only journeyed deeper into his own thoughts. Soon he whined again. "They're all running. Even that baby, rushing to nothing."

Javi stayed silent until Ian had finished his piece and his words had fully melted into the air, whisked away forever. Then he asked, "So what?"

Ian's face froze in shock. He stopped walking for a moment, before he ran to get ahead of Javi. "So what? So what!"

Javi laughed again. "Yes, that's what I said."

"How can you talk like that? How can you live like that?"

Javi stroked the side of his face. "How can you not?" Then he chuckled again. He stepped around Ian and kept walking forward. Once again, Ian dashed forward to catch up.

"Javi, stop playing games with me."

"I'm not playing games." Javi pointed up. "Look."

Ian looked up. The cloud had dissipated, revealing a pitch-black sky.

"What am I supposed to be looking at?" asked Ian.

"Give it some time," Javi said. "Let's keep walking."

Ian sighed again but continued to follow him. "How could you love that horrible woman?"

Javi laughed and raised his hands as if declaring his innocence. "I guess love works in mysterious ways." He nodded, agreeing with himself, and began to slow down. "She wasn't all bad, just scared." Then he stopped moving entirely. "We're here."

Ian looked around, violently shaking his head in his search. "Where? What's here?"

"This is where I go and you stay."

"Where?" demanded Ian. "Where are you going?"

Again, Javi shrugged. "I don't know. It's *your* dream." Then he turned to the right and walked down a new street.

Ian stood still and gawked at him. "You can't just leave!"

Javi gave him no response.

"Wait! Wait! Stay!"

Javi did not waver. He didn't turn to face his beggar, instead he said, "Ian—keep it simple. Open your eyes. Have a look around."

Javi took three more steps forward, and the entrance to a silent train car materialized in front of him. He walked in, the doors closed, and the ghost train rolled on. It started slow, began to accelerate, then slowly vanished, dissipating into nothingness as it carried its lone passenger inside. Before too long, the breeze swallowed it, and it disappeared entirely. Javi was gone.

Clutching his hair, Ian shouted, "Hello?" But across the City, only his voice echoed back to him. He was alone.

Memories bubbled up. Visions pulled on him like unstoppable weights. He fell down, but the thoughts still proved too heavy, so he dropped his back down onto the concrete. Contact brought a precise and dull pain, a cold sensation that pierced a single point on his back.

He stared up at the night sky, but there were no stars. Instead it resembled a ravenous void. In the dark, Ian could paint a weak picture of those he had met and would soon forget. It was there, in the dark night sky, for a brief and certain moment, where he saw the truth of the world as he had envisioned it.

There were those who still survived on borrowed time: Zoey, Rohan, Oscar, Lizzy, Regi, and Hallie. They all walked somewhere but did not even realize they were running out of steps. Their ignorance filled him with pity and envy.

Then there were the strangers. Those who wandered across subway stations and on desolate streets. They roamed the earth in a constant and nervous frenzy. Nearly all of them had abandoned each other. They did not speak, nor did they care to. Altogether, they created an overwhelming sea of hopes and fears, destined to fade with the wind.

And finally there were the lost, the forgotten dreamers. Ian did not even dare imagine them. He needed to bury them: forget their dreams, forget their memories, forget their faces. The three of them were gone, and the thought of finding them again created a tumultuous, self-escalating, unstoppable panic in his chest. They had been reduced to one purpose, and only one purpose. They served as a grim mirror, a reminder that all dreams end in darkness.

This was the world Ian had built for himself, both in heart and mind. For some time, it seemed he had been able to escape the density of the waking world in sleep by chasing a dream of dreams, but now reality had finally conquered dream, and he was alone.

The boy sighed, let go of his strain, and stepped into a dangerous capitulation. His body softened, his heart stalled, and his weariness overtook him. It was time to sleep, time to rest. It seemed like a fitting end to a nightmare.

However, right before Ian's eyes shuttered forever, he froze.

He stopped and stared. He could swear there was… something. Something had appeared in the night's void. Something had moved.

It was barely clear at all, more like the light of a firefly. There for a second, gone the next. He rubbed his eyes, suspecting it was his imagination, but sure enough, it happened again. Another light appeared, moved, and disappeared. Then another… and another. They all flickered into existence before they vanished forever. All in a second. Even so, when one faded, many more were born around it.

Soon the night sky was filled with fleeting lights. They moved by the thousands, all in a smooth passion. They twisted and turned around each other, flowing in unison. They grew from thousands to tens of thousands. From tens of thousands to millions. To billions. Together they spun an ever-changing story in the sky, threading their light around darkness.

And so Ian watched the infinite lights flicker as each told their own ephemeral tale, all nearly too quick to notice, a lifetime that appeared and disappeared within a second. But together, all together, they held a great shine. They roared, weaving through the sky, shifting every moment, never able to settle.

He began to cry softly. He reached toward them, wanting to touch their glow as they accelerated. At long last, he could hear their song. They sang with the relentless rumble of a blind universe. They sang to everyone, to him. He just hadn't noticed it before.

Mesmerized by the sight, he sniffled and whispered, "Okay, Javi... I see."

Both day and night, reality and dream, had taught him all things would end. Time, memory, life—they all would cease. He knew this. He had seen this.

He knew one day every flare in the sky, small and great, would fade away. Each one would be carried away into the night, and eventually no new light would join them.

But as he gazed up into the lights of the sky, he also saw all that didn't matter. Their conclusion didn't matter, their end didn't matter. The lights, for now, danced.

Ian awoke.

CHAPTER FIFTEEN

I an stretched and heard his joints moan and crack. Tenderly with his hands, he explored his back. At least two bruises and three cuts. They would need time to heal. It all ached, his back, his chest, his legs. But at least his head had cleared up.

He swung his legs off his bed and stood to face his mess. Scattered across the floor was a hodgepodge of ripped foam, wrecked ceramics, and shattered glass pieces. Carefully, he stepped around the shards and turned toward his mattress. He peered down upon it and caressed it, tracing through its foam, pits, and broken springs. There was no coming back, he realized. He had been successful. It was utterly destroyed.

Ian stared at it and contemplated lives lived before.

Then he turned, left it behind, and went to his window. He peered down at the street. He counted five strangers, each wandering on the same early morning street, breathing in the same air, feeling the same wind. Leaning over, he searched for the remnants of his phone on the floor.

The device was in poor shape, and as he picked it up, the screen's cracks cut into his thumb, but he persisted. He shoved down on the black glass, forcing it to function, forcing it to wake. After several attempts, it finally rebirthed with light.

He navigated to his contacts and painfully wrote: *Im sorry. Honest. Very sorry. Ill be at park at 5. Up to u*

Send.

He checked the window again. The street had emptied of pedestrians.

He pulled the window open to create a small opening and took another look at his phone. It had lasted three and a half years, long enough to document every detailed inch of its master, long enough to become an extension of his brain, long enough to reprogram him.

He pushed it through the slit in the window, and it fell.

It fell as another heirloom of another time gone.

It fell back to the earth that had birthed it.

It fell fast and furious and hard.

It fell whistling in the air.

It fell some more.

And then crashed onto the concrete.

Ian peered down, but he could barely see it. Up so high it was just a tiny black speck.

He proceeded to the bathroom and turned on the light. Looking in the mirror, he saw he was still a mess, with frazzled hair, dead skin, and tired eyes. He decided that was fine.

He brushed his teeth, took a shower in silence, put on his favorite clothes, stuffed a backpack, and left for the subway.

The train was sparse, with only him and two strangers— one young lady and a grizzled old man who sat at opposite sides of the car. He stepped in, approached the man, and asked, "What time is it?"

The man, snapped out his spell, looked at him, flummoxed. "You talkin' to me?"

Ian nodded. "Yes, I was wondering what time it is?"

The man pulled out his phone. "11:25."

"Thanks." He sat down, and the man peered at him before he drifted off again.

Ian's first destination filled him with dread, but he continued forth anyway. He felt a certain duty.

As he exited the train, he noticed the air wasn't cold at all. Instead it was cool, aided by a warm breeze, an early flash of spring. He passed the lone tree locked in its barricade by the end of the street. Soon enough, its leaves would return.

He entered the skyscraper that he had become so familiar with. The guard on the ground floor sized up the frazzled young man wearing street clothes, but he let him enter when Ian flashed his badge. As he rode up the elevator, Ian watched his reflection follow him along, offering him some backup as his friendly neighbor.

Then the door dinged, and he stepped out of the metal box. The woman at the office's front desk stared at him with confused surprise. He simply waved and walked on.

He was walking down the corridor when he heard, "Ian!"

Ian turned, and there was Rohan, who raced after him but stopped a few feet away. He tentatively asked, "What are you doing here, man?"

"Just saying goodbye."

"Oh."

"And I want to say I'm sorry." He watched Rohan struggle to absorb Ian's words and the situation, and Ian realized that it may have been the first fully genuine thing he had ever said to him. "Tell Zoey I'm sorry too," he added.

Rohan ruffled his hair with his hand. "I don't know what to say. I guess… You good, then?"

"Today, right now, I'm good."

"Okay. Well… good luck."

Ian managed to smile, and Rohan half-smiled back. Then, without words, they parted. Ian headed toward Oscar's office, and Rohan went back to work.

Ian knocked twice and heard: "Come in!"

He breathed slowly, took a step closer, and opened the door. Without hesitation, Oscar jumped out of his chair. "What are you doing here?"

Initially Ian struggled to speak, but eventually it became easier. Each word was born as a burden but left as bliss. "I just wanted to say... thanks. Thanks for your advice."

"Oh."

The two men looked past each other awkwardly, until Ian asked, "Can I ask you something?"

"What is it?"

"What did you want to be when you grew up? Like when you were a child."

Oscar took a moment to answer. He studied Ian, analyzing his every inch for misdirection, deceit, or just some context. But Oscar found nothing; Ian looked at him with honest eyes.

He sighed. "I guess I wanted to be an astronaut."

Ian stared at him in disbelief. He offered a chuckle as his final olive branch. "I had this old friend. I think he wanted to be an astronaut too." He turned. "Well, thanks again, Oscar. Goodbye."

As he left he heard a whispered, "Goodbye."

Ian's second destination filled him with uncertainty, but he looked forward to the result. The train carried him uptown to a refined building made of fine stone. He buzzed, waited for a moment, entered, and proceeded up the elevator.

He knocked on the gray slab of metal. His knock echoed back to him with no response, so he knocked again and heard a deep, exasperated shout. "I'M COMING!"

The door jolted open, and standing over him was Regi. In a drained voice, he asked, "Ian? What's up?"

He was in a unique state, unique for Regi. Deep gray

circles reigned under his eyes, and his entire body seemed like it could fall over and collapse at any moment.

"When's the last time you slept?" Ian asked.

That gave Regi a laugh. "It's been a couple days, I guess."

Ian peeked inside. "Is he here?"

Regi looked behind his shoulder and made an unsure face. "Yeah, we brought him home yesterday. Honestly, I don't know if this is the best time for guests, Lizzy is kind of still in the process of recovery."

Ian nodded. "I understand. Well, I just came to say goodbye."

"Goodbye? Where you going?"

"I'm not certain yet."

Regi looked at the messy man with curiosity. "I see."

Ian turned toward the elevator. "Well, bye, then. Tell Lizzy I said bye to her too."

"Yeah, see you." Regi slowly let the door begin to close before he stopped it with his foot. "Wait a minute. I'll be right back." He dashed into the apartment, and the door closed. Ian waited, staring at his shadow on the hallway wall until the door opened again.

"Here's the little guy."

In Regi's arms was a tiny little boy. He barely existed, draped in a sky-blue blanket that swallowed him whole, but when his eyes opened, Ian's heart lifted. Ian stepped closer and hovered his hand near the child. Regi nodded, and Ian took a hold of him.

Supporting his body felt strange, strange to hold this small thing, which would become something else entirely different so quickly. He grinned, sensing the child's tiny weight and soft warmth. It marked an outlandishly fantastic sensation, a beginning of the cycle, a new energy unfolding, the start of fresh time's blossoming. He held an entire world in his hands.

"What's his name?"

Regi smiled. "Reginald the Second."

Ian gaped at Regi. "Seriously?"

Regi grinned and shook his head. "No, but that's my nickname for him. It's what my mama would've wanted, I'm sure. Lizzy wanted a Benjamin. We settled on Jeremy."

"Ah," he said, as he handed back Jeremy. "Nice name."

Regi looked at his son. "I think so."

The two said their goodbyes, and Ian descended in the elevator. He walked down the street and spotted a woman rushing down the block. With the way she moved, she no doubt had somewhere to be, but he stopped her, waving her down. "Ma'am, do you know the time?"

She flinched as her brain took a moment to process the man in front of her. She pulled out her phone. "2:37."

"Thanks."

Ian decided he would take a walk.

HE WALKED BLOCK BY BLOCK. On one street, a man sat alone on a lonely stoop. On another, five children chased after each other, ducking and diving between other pedestrians, screaming all the way. On a third, a grandmother walked with her daughter and grandson.

Every block, the City changed; new ecosystems emerged every minute. He journeyed from quiet, solemn streets to massive skyscrapers and back again. He watched the countless people who passed him in all directions. Every decision of their cumulative lives had led them to that spot, with him, together, just for that moment.

He was off to his third destination. It filled him with anxiety but also gave him a loose hope, and for a final time, he watched the buildings shrink, the crowd thin, and trees bloom into sight. He had arrived in the park.

He walked down curved roads until he arrived at a

mustached man who stood behind an ice cream stand. Ian approached him and pointed to an exotic frozen lemon-lime concoction and paid the man his dues. It tasted a little like sugared grass. He proceeded down to the bike lane, parked himself on a bench, and ate his sugared grass.

Time wore on as Ian watched occasional bikers pass by and other dreamers stroll on. During his wait, he thought about things that had passed and things yet to come. They clogged his thoughts, bringing both joy and sorrow. In one way or another, the two would always be together, he decided.

After some time, he looked at the sky and saw the sun was preparing its exit. He stood and approached an older couple who were taking a walk together.

"Hello," Ian asked, "could you tell me what time it is?"

They smiled at him, and they checked their watches. "5:16," they said in unison.

Ian said his thanks and sat back down on the bench. He could wait a few more minutes. As he waited with his eyes closed, he felt a little less sunshine on his face every minute, until there was none left. Then he opened his eyes and saw the sun had sunk and day was quickly falling to night. He sighed, rose, and prepared to leave.

But after five steps, he stopped and smiled. The wait had been worth it. Shredding up the bike lane was a familiar green beanie.

Hallie came in at full speed, slammed on her brakes, and skidded to a stop in front of him. As she hopped off the bike, she said, "You must be the biggest dick in the world. You can't just declare a time to meet and then not respond." She stared at him directly on. "I have things to do. I'm not just *available* at 5."

"That makes sense," he said.

She looked away, deeper into the park, while Ian gazed at

her. He exhaled, then said, "I'm surprised you came. I'm sorry."

"Yeah, you should be sorry," she snapped back at him. "You were a dickhead."

He let the words sit for a moment before he laughed. "Yeah. I guess I was a dickhead."

She looked away again. "I'm only here 'cause I didn't want you to hurt yourself... or someone."

"Don't worry about that," he said. "I'm all good."

She raised an eyebrow. "All good? Last night you were nuts. People don't just become all good after something *like that*."

"You're probably right. What can I say? I'm all good right now, right this second, right here, right with you."

"Ian, what do you want from me?" Her voice sounded confused, dragged between frustration, anger, and pure bewilderment.

"I'm not looking for anything. I just wanted to apologize and say goodbye. I'm leaving. I got to go."

"Where are you going?"

"Somewhere else. I'm not sure yet. I may come back, but maybe not. I can't be here anymore right now. That much I know."

Hallie looked at him like she didn't know what to say but felt she should say something, so Ian spoke for her. "Just... just keep on keeping on. You're great."

"Thanks." She smirked. "I would say the same thing about you, but I don't know what the hell you're on."

Laughing again, he said, "I guess that's fair."

They stared at each other one last time before Hallie embraced him, and he embraced her. They held on to each other, anchoring one another against the world, and part of Ian wished it would never end.

After they said their goodbyes, Hallie rode off. Watching her disappear into the twilight, Ian gained a great sorrow and a great joy. She would become a memory, hopefully one sweetened by time, but a memory nonetheless. As months passed into years, she would become something entirely different than what she actually had been, a vision rewritten by lights and shadows playing tricks on his brain. At least he knew he would not forget her. And that helped him accept the fact that he would never see her again.

He weaved his way through the City via subway until he arrived back where he had started: a dark gray garage labeled *Long-Term Storage*. He journeyed to its seventh floor and found it there—his old beat-up car of a forgotten time.

He got in and started up the engine. He drove down and out into traffic. Moving in silence, with his window halfway down, he enjoyed a soft wind against his face. Perhaps he would go home, where the weather was warm and the days were long, but perhaps he wouldn't. He couldn't stay there for too long, or he might never leave.

He drove slowly, in no rush, as twilight quickly turned into night. Each dim streetlight he passed was so generous, offering him their light, their energy for his journey.

It was time to leave the City.

He had begun to turn toward an exit when everything slowed down for him. Out in the darkness of the night, with his front glass gleaming under the light of a lonely moon, his brain led him to a final epiphany. He turned around and drove to his old apartment.

Ian double-parked his car. He wouldn't be long. He hurried up the stairs and took in the space one last time. It felt strange to be back, like he had said his goodbyes, put the experiences in the back of his brain, and the memory had already begun to rot.

He opened his old door and walked back into the mess.

Nothing had changed since his departure, with yellow foam scattered around, loose springs laying all over the floor, and shards of ceramic plates ready to cut unsuspecting feet. But none of that mattered, not now and never again.

Ian turned to the ancient mattress.

Its wounds were deep and its scars apparent. Each cut extended over its surface, forming jagged crevices and ridges across its terrain. It was dead, likely entirely lost. He exhaled. He still needed to try.

He attempted to hoist the carcass onto his back, but after a single step, it was clear that would not work. Even a gentle touch brought more foam pouring out and risked destroying the entire body.

He gently put it down. Then he sat, barely feeling a bounce. Instead it gave way and pulled him down. It had lost the ability to support anyone. He rose and stared out the window at the scene he had seen for so many nights. Under a bright moon, the pedestrians continued to live their lives.

He considered running back to his car and leaving, but then he closed his eyes. It was still worth the effort.

Gently, he flipped over the mattress. On its back, it looked pure, untouched by his rage or by his weight, ready to be evaporated.

He picked up the knife he had used last night, wiped off a piece of foam on it using the windowsill, and returned to his patient.

It would need to be a perfect incision. He steadied his hand and carefully plunged the knife into the mattress's back. He formed a long rectangle over its surface and peeled off its top layer. A dusty yellow stared back at him. Then he pushed the knife deeper, into the foam, well into the hole he had built.

He dragged it along, gutting the weak body in one last attempt to salvage something. After he was finished, he had a big dirty old glob of a mattress.

The operation had been successful.

He took the glob and shaped it down to size. Then he grabbed a pillow from the floor, pulled it out of its case, and stuck the mattress glob into the empty shell. And he was gone again.

HE DROVE QUICKLY and followed familiar streets, recalling a bus path. The pillow sat in the seat next to him, and occasionally he glanced at it. It was not much of a pillow, more like a flat square pad. It would have to be enough.

He had dug back into the mattress's deepest pit, back to its earliest life, back when there was only the first dreamer, its first sleeper, a hopeful brother. Maybe it would carry a dream. He prayed that it would be a good one.

Finally, he saw it. The modest white building with the words *Albin Elder Care Institute* proudly displayed. He clutched the pillow against his chest and approached its front door. He pulled on the handles, but it did not budge. Inside was pitch black, locked down.

He began to trace the building's outside. Checking and rechecking the view behind him, he counted four—no, five— windows down from the right side of lobby. His guess would have to be right. He stuffed the pillow under his shirt, took a few steps back, ran, and desperately jumped.

With his arms fully stretched, he barely managed to grab the windowsill's ledge. He pushed his feet against the stone and pressed his body against the wall to keep the pillow from falling. Using all of his remaining strength, he hoisted himself up with one hand and held the pillow in the other. Then, sitting on a ledge, he opened up the window, dumped himself inside, and approached her. *Adriana.*

The moon's shine embraced her face, bringing back some long-lost glow, but the beautiful moment didn't last long. As she rolled in her sleep, she twitched her head back and forth, constantly bringing herself in and out of the light from the window.

Breathing quietly, Ian took the pillow out from under his shirt. He thought he must look ridiculous, but it didn't matter. If he could only give her a second, a moment, it would be worth it.

He tiptoed over and pulled up Adriana's head and pillow. She began to shake harder, terrified in her sleep, so he stopped. He didn't want to wake her. Instead he sat on the floor and felt the coolness of its tiles against his clothes. There, waiting for her, he listened to her shallow breaths and her bed's creaks, her torment. Closing his eyes, he thought about how he was likely one of the last connections to her being, to her story. The thread that tethered her life to the world's memory had become slim, wispy. Almost nonexistent. But he would hold it.

He exhaled. The sounds had subsided; she had stilled.

He rose, tipped up her pillow and head. He could sense her weight, or the lack of it. She had become so small, so frail, and yet she could feel so much pain.

He placed the pillow, the pad, the progeny, under her head, hidden in plain sight, and was done. Carefully, he laid her head back down and walked to the window. Before he jumped out, he turned to face her one last time. He would forever swear to himself that he saw the thinnest outline of a smile.

CHAPTER SIXTEEN

I an drove, wandering into the dark. Perhaps he would wander forever. The moon's glare lit his dashboard and guided him forward. Outside of the city, the night sky's simple lights, its moon and faint stars, combined to create brilliance. Beside him, rows of dark trees swooshed against the breeze, and humble grass hugged the earth.

There was silence and there was peace. And in this peace, the night brought back familiar thoughts, familiar dreams to swirl in the young man's head.

Somewhere in the city, Rohan, Zoey, and Oscar would be all home. They would be smiling, embracing their loves, letting another day sink into night. He pictured Regi and Lizzy holding little Jeremy tight in their arms, enjoying his warmth and sweet smell. And somewhere far away, Hallie rode on to another adventure. They would forget about him; they all would forget him. That was true, but it was what it was.

Still, one vision was harder to accept. As Ian stared into the night, one rang above the rest. Brighter, louder than all their voices, than all their dreams, than all their lives, was the quiet flow of a river. In the black of a true night, it was the clearest it had ever been, and he could see inside its steady stream of light and sound. It reflected back the smile of a girl and rebounded the laugh of her brother. Driving alone, he could see them, he could feel them.

They were gone, that was true. But at least he would remember them. He must remember.

His heart began to burn, to turn, with things that had been lost and would not be found. Images leapt across his mind, dreams unfulfilled, times gone. They plunged themselves into his consciousness, filling everything, until they were all he could see.

But he stopped them.

He should be satisfied, he told himself. He would be their keeper. Driving into the dark, he forced himself to smile. He tried to rediscover the day's warm breeze and enjoy the night's quiet. He had reached peace, he decided.

Then he closed his window and turned on the radio. For a moment, the wind had gone cold again.

ACKNOWLEDGMENTS

This novel would have never reached its full potential without the support, feedback, and wisdom of my family, friends, and mentors.

Specifically I'd like to thank:
    My editors, Crystal Watanabe and Michele Ford
    My book cover artist, Bailey McGinn
    Ma (Elayne Kesselman)
    Kate Kesselman
    Matthew Hertz
    Austin Cheng
    Elizabeth Hobbs
    Graham Barbour
    Michael Bloom
    Alexander Brinkley
    Mike DeVries
    Kaitlyn Early
    Phineas Morgan Alexander
    Cindy Dale
    Deonte Hall

Daniel Lowe
Cynthia DiPaula
Ian Gallagher
Tommy Luo

Additional thanks to those who helped review the novel's cover:
Payson Burnett
Meredith Callahan
Nikita Eliseev
David Jacobs
Bryce McCarthy
Nia Meressa
Lauren Ott
Nyasia Rhine
Kevin Vellanki
Zabih Yousuf

And most of all thank you, my reader

Dear Reader,

Thanks again for reading *Buried Vapors*. I hope it was a worthwhile experience.

If you want to help me further (or warn the masses), please don't hesitate to leave a review on Amazon or Goodreads. It's the best way for authors with small publishers to gain exposure.

Additionally, feel to visit my website matthewkesselman.com or my YouTube channel, if you would be interested in any of my future work. There's plenty of exciting projects to come. And reach out! I love interacting with my readers.

Lastly, I hope your life is going a little more smoothly than Ian's, and is getting better and better every day.

All the best,

Matthew

Made in the USA
Columbia, SC
08 July 2020